BLUE BEAR
WOMAN

We gratefully acknowledge the support of the Canada Council for the Arts and the Ontario Arts Council for our publishing program. We also acknowledge the financial support of the Government of Canada.

Cover design: Val Fullard

Library and Archives Canada Cataloguing in Publication

Title: Blue bear woman : a novel / Virginia Pesemapeo Bordeleau ; translated by Susan Ouriou & Christelle Morelli. Other titles: Ourse bleue. English
Names: Pésémapéo Bordeleau, Virginia, 1951- author. |
Ouriou, Susan, translator. | Morelli, Christelle, translator.
Series: Inanna poetry & fiction series. Description: Series statement: Inanna poetry & fiction series | Translation of: Ourse bleue
Identifiers: Canadiana (print) 20190147873 | Canadiana (ebook) 20190147881 | ISBN 9781771336819 (softcover) | ISBN 9781771336826 (epub) | ISBN 9781771336833 (Kindle) | ISBN 9781771336840 (pdf)
Classification: LCC PS8631.E797 O9713 2019 | DDC C843/.6—dc23

Printed and bound in Canada

Inanna Publications and Education Inc.
210 Founders College, York University
4700 Keele Street, Toronto, Ontario, Canada M3J 1P3
Telephone: (416) 736-5356 Fax: (416) 736-5765
Email: inanna.publications@inanna.ca Website: www.inanna.ca

FSC
www.fsc.org
MIX
Paper from
responsible sources
FSC® C004071

BLUE BEAR WOMAN

Virginia Pesemapeo Bordeleau

translated by

Susan Ouriou & Christelle Morelli

inanna poetry & fiction series

INANNA PUBLICATIONS AND EDUCATION INC.
TORONTO, CANADA

*For my children, my grandchildren,
and my entire family*

The universe is a deeply moving enigma: as soon as I begin to delve further, I feel more alive. Despite all the still unanswered questions.
                                    —Joseph Gaarder

What does our life here on earth resemble? A flock of crows, alighting on snow and leaving the occasional imprint of their claws.
                                    —Su Dong Po

PART I
THE JOURNEY TO JAMES BAY

*They are wise who do not let reality
disrupt their dreams.*
—Christiane Singer

1

JOS AND ALLAISY
AUGUST 2004

THIS MORNING, we set out for James Bay. I have no idea the journey will lead me to obscure territories hidden deep in impenetrable atavistic memories. The dream that pulled me from sleep was most likely a warning.... In it, Daniel and I tour a church.

Peculiar its architecture, somewhere between medieval and modern. On the altar in the centre is Christ on his wooden cross. A lever protrudes from the granite flagstone in the floor. Daniel reaches out to see how it works. My warning comes too late. He's already pulling the handle toward him. Immediately, the flagstones beneath our feet begin to shift. I grab Daniel's arm and cry, "Follow me!" Without waiting, I run through the wide open doors. The steps pull free one after another behind me, my feet barely touching them. Certain that my husband follows close behind, I only look back once I've tumbled into the arms of my brother, Maikan, who stops me in my tracks. A terrified crowd witnesses the church's collapse. But Daniel isn't behind me. I see his hand, his ring hand, emerge from the pile of rubble. I cry out both in my dream and in bed as my worried spouse shakes me.

The morning begins with a timid sun hiding behind clouds. July's heat is behind us and mosquitoes have grown scarce by day. To be on the safe side, we buy fruit, vegetables, rice, pasta, and packaged sauce in Amos. Red wine. We'll eat off picnic tables and sleep in the van or tent.

We stop at a few interpretive signs the tourist bureau has labelled "*Les voix de la voie du Nord*"—Voices of the Northern Route. Mining sites. A lake with emerald waters. An esker. The afternoon hours tick by. We keep an eye out for a place for our evening meal. I'd like a discreet location, a lake to bathe in. At the crossroads to Joutel, a former mining town, we admire the view of distant hills. A few people are busy consulting a road map spread out on the hood of their car. A woman laughs loudly. Not that anyone is in danger of getting lost here since there's only one road to follow.

Behind the steering wheel, Daniel waits for a Matagami-bound truck to pass. Across the road, I see a sign: *Camping sauvage*. I touch his arm and nod at the sign for wilderness camping. He smiles, crosses the road, and drives up a wide sandy path. A chain link fence surrounds the spot, but the gate is open. Through jack pines, we see a lake. We make our way to the empty campsites and crumbling fire pits invaded by pine and birch regrowth. We like the site and its ruggedness. I shed my clothes and slip into my swimsuit. The cold water invigorates me and I push through a few lengths, humming to give me strength.

A shout, somewhere between astonishment, incredulity and joy, sounds from shore. It's Daniel calling me. I wade out of the water and am immediately swarmed by mosquitoes. Daniel stands by the picnic table, his hands full of chanterelles. My favourite mushroom! "And this is nothing!" he says. He parts the bushes to reveal the gleam of not just a multitude of saffron-capped chanterelles, but lobster mushrooms, too.

That evening, the mosquitoes give chase. We light a fire in the firepit that we feed with green grasses. The thick smoke gives us some respite as we prepare to dry our harvest. "Thanks be to Kitchi Manitou!" Daniel says. We have no idea that we've just entered nature's fast food court and that we will have many more occasions to thank the Great Spirit.

A dream. A friend asks me to smudge her house haunted by

a spirit. There are no windows, no light. I'm not sure I'll be able to help. Daniel shoves me with his behind and I wake up. With the van parked on an incline, I've been rolling into him all night long. Because of that incline, I'll remember the dream.

The rising sun throws the pine trees' long shadows across the small lake by the road. We can already hear transport trucks driving by. The coffee gives off an enticing smell and I make a mushroom omelet. Meanwhile, my husband explores our surroundings. He discovers the relics of a large well-appointed campground with concrete foundations, tumbledown buildings, and an old playground. It's as though I can hear the joyous cries of vacationing families in the wind brushing past. Where there are mines, cities are born then die. Men and women harbour the hope that the earth's womb will provide gold or copper in perpetuity. The seam runs out. So hope is abandoned, to be buried and left behind, eyes averted. In sorrow.

We drive another few kilometres and enter Matagami. Some forty years ago, before the city was built, my mother's cousin Jos Domind, his wife Allaisy, and their many children had their trapping grounds here. Before the James Bay Agreement. Trees were felled and foundations dug, and that was that. An Algonquin reserve farther south welcomed Jos and Allaisy. No more trapping or hunting. They grew old.

In a local paper, we read that Matagami is dying. With the mine's closing, the government has announced logging restrictions. Word has it that forests are truly thinning, it's no longer just a rumour. Jos and Allaisy's spirits still roam this vast territory, as do their parents' and grandparents' roots. Forty years have passed and new inhabitants quake at the thought of their precarious toehold. They hope for a diamond mine.

We leave our names and addresses at the municipality's tourist information bureau. Safety first. Soon a sign warns: "Remote road, continue at your own risk." We're being told to exercise extreme caution. Here I've come to look in on the country of my Cree origins, and I'm being warned of danger.

I'm torn between laughter and scorn. I touch the medicine bag hanging around my neck. My anger dissipates.

The promised solitude galvanizes us. The murmur of an inner voice evokes the untamed beauty of a land to be discovered, a space to drink in with all our being, its breath to be woven into the days and nights to come. Suddenly, we're happy.

We realize it's our anniversary. Today. We stop on the shores of Lake Matagami. The wind is so strong we have to anchor the corners of the tablecloth with stones. We open a bottle of red wine in our honour and drink to Jos and Allaisy's spirit and to their huge lake.

The main purpose of our trip is to meet up with Carolynn, my mother's aunt, in Nemaska. She is the only survivor of that generation who still has memories of the Cree grandfather I never knew. We're nearing the road to Waskaganish where my grandmother Louisa and great-uncle George were born. An artist friend lives here whom we hope to see as well. Maybe we should drive straight to Nemaska and visit my great-aunt first? Mulling over the choices, we admire the lichen and moss under the jack pines. Suddenly, out of the bush to the right, a black shape looms. My palms sweating on the wheel, I slow down. The good-sized bear crosses the road and runs some hundred metres ahead of us. By the Waskaganish intersection, it vanishes in the direction of the village. Daniel winks at me. I signal a left turn.

2

FRANCES AND JOSEPH
JULY 1960

SITTING UNDER THE SHADE of a grove of leafy birch trees, Maman prepares lunch over her summer fire. She always complains about the heat coming from the wood-burning stove. Perspiration runs down her face, wiped away periodically with a corner of her skirt cut from a large swath of flowered cotton and sewn by hand. Butter melts in the iron pan balanced on stones.

I shoo away the flies hovering by the fillets of walleye and northern pike caught by our parents overnight in a net strung along the bottom of the Nottaway River. We name the waterways in the language of the territory. The Nottaway runs the length of the village across the way, then flows into Shabogama Lake farther down. Papa says, *"Les garçons, nous construirons un bateau que nous appellerons* Shabogama…"

Maman asks what he's on about. She laughs. *"Josep, tchi tchish kwan…."*

My father laughs in turn. He likes to tease her by speaking to his children in French, the language she doesn't understand. Today is a day of peace and quiet, a haven of calm for our hearts, of warm light. As its juices combine with the butter, the fish sizzles and spatters, burning Maman's hand.

She reaches for an old towel to cover the handle. My father grabs the axe and starts splitting a birch log. My mother raises the pan of fish to let him add wood splinters to the flames. With an air of complicity, they exchange a look born of their life together and their feelings for each other. Maman serves the boys their portion, warning them to eat slowly and watch for fishbones. Famished, my oldest brother doesn't wait. He drops his dish, coughs, chokes. His red face grimaces from the strain. His eyes fill with tears.

Maman jumps to her feet and pounds on Jimmy's back. She yells "N'Goussish! N'Goussish!" and forces Jimmy to open wide so she can insert her plump finger still oily with cooking grease inside.

Jimmy gurgles, "Aaaargh...." Tragedy in their eyes, the little ones think he's dying. They shiver in the sunshine. Calm is restored when Jimmy coughs up the fishbone.

My father hands him some bannock. I take it upon myself to check for any bones overlooked in the fillets on each of my little brothers' metal plates since they've stopped eating and are eyeing their portions warily. It does look like Jimmy was the only one treated to a bone.

Makwashish, Little Bear, my second youngest brother named for his thick head of black hair, keeps imitating his brother's cry. Clutching his neck with both hands, he groans, "Eurghh...." Then points at Jimmy.

The baby, asleep in her makeshift hammock slung between two trees, wakens to the din of conversation around Jimmy's fishbone. She whimpers, still drowsy. My father picks up his daughter and rocks her as he waits for his wife to finish her meal. He says, "Sibi's unleashed a river again." His nickname for her is "Rivière" because he claims she pees like one.

My mother pulls off her blouse soaked with milk leaking from her breasts. She folds her top, lays it in the crook of her left arm to nestle her naked baby's head there and, bare-chested in the summer's light, she nurses Sibi. Her copper skin glistens with sweat. In one swift motion, my father dips the towel into a pan of cool water and wipes down my mother's body. After an initial start, she sighs with pleasure. Next he lifts up her hair and pins it to the top of her head with the bobby pins she uses to keep her face free. He pats down her neck and shoulders front and back.

After the baby's feed, Maman spreads a blanket out in the shade of the birch trees and fetches her beading bag from our cabin. She settles in comfortably, her thimble on her middle finger, multicoloured beads spread out in a saucer. One by one, she strings them onto her needle. She's beading moose-hide moccasins for me for the coming winter. "You'll check the traps with your father on weekends...."

I lie down beside her on my back. Through the leaves, I see contrails left by an airplane, so far away they're barely visible. I say, "One day, I'll fly in a plane like that..." Maman looks up and a glimmer of panic flashes through her dark eyes.

"Don't say that, Ikwesis, your words could come true!" Maman has taken seaplanes, trains, cars. But, being an unknown, international air carriers come under the realm of witchcraft.

Her voice softens and she says, "I dreamt of you last night. The dream must have scared me because your father had to shake me awake. I was screaming in my sleep. You were sitting on a *Mist Pishou*, like the ones that live on *Maktesinabech* land!" She means a lion. That lives in the land of black men.

"Do you mean I was riding it like a horse?"

"That's right.... You were clinging to its mane as it raced full-tilt ahead. I yelled for it to leave you alone or for you to let go, but you couldn't hear me. It was running so fast. What will become of you, *n'danch?* That dream scares me. As though it's not enough that when you were little, your dreams sometimes showed you things you could never have seen...."

I don't want to hear her worries. "*Nigawi,* tell me about the time Koukoum Louisa ate too many blueberries!"

She looks up from her beading, smiles, then laughs outright. Just then, two of my younger brothers fall onto us, caught up in one of their daily fights. With a moccasin in her hand, Maman swats at her sons crying, "Shoo, shoo!" as though they were two sled dogs. Flanked by the two youngest, aged four and two, my father drops the paddle he's been carving and runs to separate the combattants. He grabs each one by the belt and lifts them up like featherweights. Philou and Demsy keep kicking and throwing punches in mid-air.

Now high spirits carry the day. The ridiculous scene has the littlest ones rolling on the ground laughing hysterically. Held at knee height in their father's firm grip, the enemy brothers, at first crimson with rage, are now hiccuping as they stifle their giggles. Choking with laughter, Jimmy wipes his eyes with his shirt sleeve.

Then calm returns, brightened by the chirping of birds in the trees. One by one, the children grow drowsy and find a nearby spot for a nap. That's when, softly, Maman tells me the tale of the grandmother who gorged herself on blueberries.

"It was September. We were on our way to our trapping grounds. You were born that hot, sunny summer. Your grandparents came along and your great-uncle George, my mother's brother, and his family. We took three canoes and towed a fourth full of winter provisions. We'd be paddling and camping for at least a fortnight." She stops, lost in memories of a happy, companionable, nostalgic past.

"One day, it might have been our third day out, we canoed down a branch of the river looking for a good spot to camp for the night. It was late afternoon. On every side stood blueberry bushes heavy with ripe berries. For quite some time, we'd been hearing muffled grunting and groaning. We knew it must be a bear feeding on the many berries. We paddled in silence. Then, at a bend in the river, we caught sight of Noumoushoum, Grandfather Bear, full to bursting with fruit. He rolled on his back, groaning in pain, his big paws clutching his aching belly. Seeing him, your koukoum burst out laughing. We have a great deal of respect for the bear, who's our ancestor according to our legends. But your grandmother couldn't help laughing at the greedy creature's plight."

My mother laughs silently, reliving the episode and what was to come. "We stopped sooner than planned to pick blue-berries. We had to make do with handful after handful of the blueberries for supper that day. In the middle of the night, your father and I woke to moaning not unlike the bear's. I grabbed the flashlight and your father the shotgun. Without waking either Jimmy or you, we stepped outside. The groaning was coming from your grandparents' tent lit by a kerosene lantern.

"My uncle George and his wife Julia followed on our heels, curious and worried. Sound asleep, their children hadn't budged. We announced our presence and pulled back the tent flaps. A stench of vomit wafted through the air. Sitting next to your prostate grandmother was my step-father, busy wiping her forehead with a wet cotton cloth. He seemed torn between his concern and a desire to laugh. To me, he said, 'Noumoush-oum Mackwa has punished your mother for making fun of him....' Indeed, lying on her side, my mother clutched her stomach with both hands and groaned, a basin by her head. Despite her suffering, we couldn't help but laugh. Showing her sense of humour, Koukoum rolled back and forth on her back, imitating the bear's sounds and actions, a victim of her own overindulgence."

The story enlivened their evenings all that following winter. Miming a stomachache, Grandmother Louisa would exaggerate all the moaning and groaning to cut short the clan's teasing.

3

STANLEY AND JUDAH
AUGUST 2004

R AIN TODAY. The sun shines through a curtain of drops.
I drive slowly along the gravel road. We encounter vans
coming toward us with Cree drivers at the wheel. They slow
as we approach and stare. I recognize this attitude to strangers. We drive through a territory ravaged by fire. From their
grey, naked branches, dead trees, still standing, watch their
skinny offspring's struggle to climb hills of rock worn down
by ancient glaciers.

In the distance, a radiant mist rises, illuminated by a half
rainbow. We're nearing Waskaganish—a damp, full-bodied
scent reaches our nostrils. It's as though nature is welcoming
us. My Cree grandfather's name was, after all, Cord of the
Sun.... I like to think that my ancestors, their emblem the bear,
guide our journey north. We emerge onto a vast prairie of wild
golden grasses leading to the village's first houses.

We book a room in an inn built of huge logs that faces the
Rupert River. A man is busy vacuuming the lobby. Sand has
infiltrated everywhere. The clerk at the reception desk asks if
I'm Cree. I say, *"Egoudeh!"* and show her my Department of
Indian Affairs card. She gives me a rebate equal to the amount
of the tax. The smell of fried food wafts through the hallways.
We pass laughing guests on their way to the restaurant.

I don't want to see anyone tonight. Instead, I want to walk
along the riverbank, feel and encounter the spirit of Koukoum
Louisa's birthplace. Splintered boats lie abandoned on the

shore, overrun with wild grasses and shrubs. We head back to the village and stroll through the streets. Rain has dug deep furrows in the sandy soil. Tire tracks have swerved through people's yards to avoid certain ruts. Built in a row like urban suburbs down south, bungalows have taken over where log cabins and tents used to stand. In alleys, tipis serve as smoke-houses for small game.

Children play, race up to us on bikes, screech to a stop, and ask who we are. Surprised to hear me answer them in their language, their eyes crinkle in mirth and they wave good-bye before tearing downhill.

After a shower, we finish the bottle of wine from lunch with the cheese Daniel thought to put in the picnic basket. Using his left hand, he's clumsy unbuttoning my pyjama top. We laugh at a stubborn button then fall, legs and arms entwined, onto the double bed. Tomorrow we'll stop by the Band Council office to ask after my friend Brad and visit some must-see sights with him. I hope he's in the vicinity.

Our neighbours open and slam doors. We can hear them laughing, talking in loud voices or shushing each other just as loudly. They come and go from one room to the next. I recognize the Cree exuberance. We clearly don't live on the same schedule.

My thoughts break away to my early childhood. In the summer months, several Cree and Algonquin families would pitch their tents on a point of land not far from where we lived. Pointe-aux-Vents. We squatted there year-round. That summer my father, hired to help build the new National Defence base on a neighbouring hill, felt the desire to settle down in one place. A shady path led to the camp. Every summer, we loved being reunited with my grandmother and her second husband, our cousins and friends. My mother was strict about my sticking close to home, unless friends came to fetch me. Knowing I'd want to sleep over in their tents, her greatest fear was the lice I might—and did at times—catch at certain friends' places.

Her cousins liked us children, proud to have Métis relatives. They saw another kind of beauty in our mixed skin tone and curly hair.

One day, having escaped my mother's vigilance, I headed for Jos and Allaisy's tent. The stove was lit because of a chill in the air. I had come to play with Alice, a second cousin my age. Lying down, a hand on his wife's knee, Jos whispered to her, "Hey, here's La Toute Petite—the Little Little One—Tititèche." The tenderness in his voice had a quality that reminds me of my shyness back then: he spoke softly, as though not to spook a young animal.

I perched on the stump at the entrance to their tent. *"Tan'te Alisse...?* " Where's Alice? As with every other time I spoke to an adult, both Jos and Allaisy burst out laughing. What mistake had I made this time?

As I hurried off, Allaisy called me back, *"Astum, Iskwech...!"* Come back, my girl.... Eventually, I'd learn they couldn't wrap their heads around the fact that I could speak two Indigenous languages, yet knew nothing of either French or English. In their eyes, I was neither Cree, nor Algonquin, or white.

Suddenly, I'm aware of a sorrow that has lain dormant. I miss those people. I could never get enough of their friendly presence. In spite of myself, silent tears fall onto the pillow. Daniel snores through the hubbub in the inn. I wait for silence to reign before falling asleep. Around midnight, I hear a dog yapping then howling. Exhausted, I close my eyes and dive into a deep sleep.

A dream. A man struggles to free himself from bushes imprisoning him like real arms. A soft glow forms a huge cone hovering above him, never quite touching him. He seems to want to reach out to the light, but he's paralyzed. I can feel his anguish and want to help but am incapable of moving. Then I hear him say, "Your name is Humbert, you are a king of the nomads, and I am George." Even in my dream, I know that I'm dreaming and try—desperately—to make sense of it all.

Just then, Daniel gets up and opens the curtains. Faint grey light penetrates the room. It's early yet. The dog is still yapping. Daniel tells me the creature kept him up for part of the night. Thanks to the dog, the dream will be etched in my memory.

We leave the silent inn to get some fresh air and make coffee with our camping gear. We'll have breakfast in the restaurant later on this morning. Suddenly, Daniel squeezes my arm and points at a magnificent golden eagle straight overhead. Hunting. Soaring on the wind, guided by currents of air. I shout out, "The symbol of the Great Spirit himself, wow—hold onto your tuque, hon!"

At the reception desk in the Band Council office, I learn with surprise that Brad actually works there. The young employee in blue jeans and an embroidered white blouse butchers my name over the phone. She hands the receiver to me. My friend's warm voice reassures me.

He shows up immediately. He's put on weight. We laugh over that. I introduce him to my husband. Brad knows three languages, but speaks to us in French. He announces that he'll soon be a first-time father. He's so thrilled his round face lights up and his black eyes sparkle. Although he's happy that we've dropped by, he can't get away right now to show us around. He suggests we meet with the village's genealogists. Turning to me, he asks in Cree, "Wouldn't you like to know the names of your great-great-grandparents?" I'm taken off guard. Brad asks the receptionist to tell Tom and Stanley that we're on our way.

He invites us to follow him over to some buildings that look more like an airport hangar than a museum. Yet it is a museum according to a sign hanging on the wall inside the entrance. The door swings in the wind. Brad pulls back a thick cotton curtain hanging from shower rings attached to hooks in the ceiling. At the back of the room are two similar curtains making it look as though we're standing in a huge tent.

We cross another space inhabited by the past. Objects on the walls call to mind images of Vikings. Ship anchors. Whale harpoons. Others bear witness to the long association between the Hudson's Bay Company's factors and the Cree. Someone has gone to the trouble of collecting these relics.

Brad peers over a low wall behind which a high-pitched voice sounds. A slim man with white hair and cheerful eyes emerges. He's wearing a bright red sweater. Tom, the museum's head curator, is an American. Brad asks him if I could be given access to documents pertaining to my family.

Just then, the double curtains are pulled back and a Cree man, who wears his hair long, and a boy enter. The man is in charge of the genealogical portion of the museum. His name tells me we could very well be distant cousins. Stanley Domind. He can't place my grandmother in his family lineage because Louisa is such a common name among the Cree.

"She had a brother, George...."

Stanley stares intently, suddenly serious. His brown hands sweep the air around him. "So we're cousins then," he says in Cree, "George was my grandfather."

I'm flooded with emotion. I don't dare ask him what he knows of his ancestor, so familiar for so long. Without a word, he pulls a thick document from a metal filing cabinet. Coloured bookmarks stick out from the pages. He snaps the volume open and points at our family tree. The first ancestor at the top of the page bears the name Judah Ntayumin. My understanding is that the surname stands for *N'dai min,* the heart berry—strawberry in Cree—a name later deformed into *Domind* by Scottish and English missionaries and traders. Stanley corrects me. He pronounces the name slowly through full lips to allow me to read and listen at the same time. "*Nede ni yu min* or it is as I speak...." It takes me a few seconds to recognize it as our family's surname, "It Is As I Speak," namely, "I Walk My Words."

For the space of an instant, I dimly hear my heart pounding, a drum. I gather into every fibre of my being the true name that my grandmother bore. As did Great-Uncle George. Aware of a sacred moment, Stanley adds softly, "Our ancestors were a people of the word. Wise men and women."

After many minutes during which I hear Daniel and Tom murmuring behind us, I ask, "Do you realize that the first known ancestor's name was Judah. That sounds like Judas. His full name was Judah I Walk My Words. How telling! The traitor who keeps his word! Quite the contract!"

My second cousin smiles, amused, and scoffs gently at my surprise. "It is, in fact, quite a droll ... and limiting surname. Hah! But what about you, other than being my cousin, who are you, what do you do?"

We talk at length about different branches of the family. The numerous Nedeniyumin-become-Domind offspring, whose daughters followed their spouses to other communities—Nemaska, Waswanipi, Mistissini.... Bonds grown distant over time but kept alive through the oral tradition and syllabics.

4

KOUKOUM KA WAPKA OOT
JULY 1961

TODAY WE'RE CELEBRATING Demsy's sixth birthday. His name is actually George. Maman made a cake from scratch with chocolate icing. We can't wait to dig into the only cake we'll have all summer, other than mine in August, because the stove heats our poorly insulated log house way too much. My little brother cuts us tiny portions, giving rise to loud cries of protest on our part. Maman urges him to be more generous. He says, "I want to keep some for Koukoum; she's on the train."

Just then, we hear the far-off whistle of the locomotive warning of its arrival at a crossing. Angry at what she sees as a lie, Maman scolds him, "Stop talking nonsense, you know your grandmother's dead!" An offended Demsy picks up the miniature cars he received as gifts and heads out to line them up in the sandbox, leaving his piece of cake untouched.

Soon after, a taxi climbs the hill to our house. Like a flock of birds propelled by curiosity, we rush out to greet our visitors. There is only one. Fuelled by the same delight, we cry, "Koukoum Ka Wapka Oot!" Philou is the first to race inside and tell our mother. Sensitive Demsy stands in the sandbox, a toy car in each hand, and stares in our direction, frowning at how unfairly he's been treated. Grandmother Who Wears Glasses digs happily into a large piece of his birthday cake.

Koukoum Ka Wapka Oot's first name is the same as her sister-in-law's, our grandmother Louisa Domind. She married Noah, Koukoum's older brother. Since her husband's death, she has lived with the family founded by her son Willy, who married an Algonquin woman and traps in the Oskalaneo region only accessible by train. She'd visit us, unannounced at times, and set up her tent in the shade of the trees around the perimeter of our land. We loved her stays. Our grandmother meant an adult presence, something we could be deprived of for days at a time because of our parents' sporadic disappearances.

Koukoum Ka Wapka Oot's face, like leather weathered by use, radiated joy. Short, skinny and straight-backed, she walked with the help of a stick. She invariably wore a large flowered scarf on her head, summer and winter alike, so we had never seen the colour of her hair. Her skin colour, verging on black, had earned her the nickname *Koukoum Ka Maktesitt,* Grandmother Who is Black. Gifted with an unbelievable storyteller's talent—using the ideal tone, dramatic pauses, appropriate sound effects—her voice pulled us along in her wake until well after dark, like ducklings paddling in single file behind their mother. Seated around her mattress, we waited quietly and patiently for a story she'd made up or a traditional one from our culture. Sometimes she told a true story become a fable, like the one about the man who, in a time of famine, killed and ate his whole family. He turned into an ogre, a *koukoudji,* and Grandmother Domind made him so real that we could sense him outside prowling around her tent.

Sometimes during fall visits, she'd sleep at the foot of my bed. With her old body accustomed to hard surfaces, she refused with a laugh the bed offered out of concern for her. Despite her age, her teeth, sharp and pointed like a weasel's, were still healthy and white.

During this particular stay, my mother and her aunt told us about our great-uncle George, Ka Wapka Oot's brother-in-law. In their telling, his disappearance during a trapping expedition took on mythic proportions. The only proof of our mother's uncle's existence is one black-and-white photograph. A dozen Cree and Algonquin look out at us—pretty women, young and old, a few men. My grandmother, her brother George, my mother. A plaid *tikinagan* leans against my mother's legs, a fair-skinned child inside swaddled in pale cloth. Maman kept me protected from the sun so my skin would stay pale.

Grandmother Who Is Black unpacks large cotton bags of provisions and unwraps dried moose meat from butcher's paper. The tough jerky serves as a snack for nomads on the move. Each morsel has to be chewed at length before it can be swallowed. Since our mother has quit preserving game the old way, Koukoum gives us an opportunity to taste traditional food. She's amused by the little ones' reluctance to try what they call *mistik wass*. Wood meat.

Our mother cooks hare stew on her summer campfire. She talks to Koukoum, who mentions Demsy's birthday. "Was it your uncle's first name you gave him?"

Maman answers, "Yes and no. You know young Queen Elizabeth? Josep is fond of her. We called our first son Charlie in honour of Elizabeth's eldest, Charles. There was also my brother Charly, you knew him, he died of tuberculosis. The name is bad luck...."

A moment's silence. Koukoum waits. She clears her throat.

My mother continues, "Our second son is named after Prince Philip, and George after Elizabeth's father...."

Koukoum laughs, "A real family of *Mista Okimatch*." Great Chiefs.

Flattered, Maman smiles. She adores her sons, the four still living from her marriage to my father and the eldest, Jimmy, who never knew his father. As soon as our summer holidays are over, Jimmy will leave for the Indian residential school in Saint-Marc-de-Figuery. As for us, we'll go to the village school on a yellow bus every morning as fall approaches.

Suddenly intense, Koukoum says in a husky voice, "He was never found...." The two women look sad, lost in thought.

Always eager for a story, I forget my manners and interrupt the grown-ups. "Who're you talking about?"

Maman glances at her aunt, a question in her eyes. Her aunt nods.

Grandmother realizes she has a new story to tell and a glimmer of contentment crosses her wrinkled features. She darts her small pink tongue back and forth over her lips. Her tongue contrasts with the dark of her skin and reminds me of our cat Pishou. Koukoum ponders how best to broach the disappearance of her brother-in-law George. We'll soon learn that the tragedy still lives on in their hearts and memories.

An impatient Philou snatches a toy car out of Demsy's hand. Demsy immediately reacts, punching him on the shoulder. They both start hollering. Annoyed, Koukoum threatens to stop talking if they don't quit fighting. Fed up, Maman pulls Philou to her, keeping a firm grip on him. Demsy huddles next to Ka Wapka Oot, protecting himself from any other attacks his brother might launch. Maikanshish or Ti-Loup—Little Wolf—four years old, always the mediator, walks over to Philou and holds out his hand. Philou doesn't understand at first, then realizes his brother wants him to hand over the car for Demsy. He gives him the toy, but promises himself to settle his score with his brother later on.

"George, your great-uncle, was the youngest in his family. His father Mathew and mother Mary separated for five years. When they got back together, they had two other children—Louisa and George. In all, eight of their children survived. So fortunate.... Children are gifts from Miste Man'tou. When they're in good health, they provide support to their parents and clan. Mathew died before his wife, Mary. George was sixteen. Already a good hunter, he provided for his mother over her remaining years. When he married, his wife, a generous woman, soon grew fond of her mother-in-law."

So began our encounter with our great-uncle. Today I can see that my mother, hurt by the recent, successive losses of her brother, her son, her uncle, and her mother, had avoided speaking to us of their deaths. But anything was possible when

Koukoum Who Is Black opened her imaginary box. Even our mother let herself be won over.

An account written by a missionary who worked with the Cree describes the Cree people as tall, of good build, and lovers of palaver. Palaver as in "an idle, never-ending discussion." Most likely, the missionary was describing an exercise in democracy that still takes place today in our communities, where each member takes all the time needed to illustrate his or her viewpoint. Koukoum initiated us into the world of palaver. With limited success.

She does, however, return to the subject of her brother-in-law George, gone one winter day to check his traps during a harsh period of starvation. He hoped to bring home a few beaver, grown scarce because of overhunting. Their fur, sought after at the time, allowed the family to survive by trading with the Hudson's Bay Company. For flour, sugar, salt, bullets, fabric. The fatty, nourishing beaver meat added protein to the Crees' frugal diet.

George never returned.

After an absence that lasted several days, his worried family sent men out to follow his tracks. They came back empty-handed with strange stories to tell....

Thrilled at our expectant gaze as we listen, Koukoum begins to speak more and more slowly. We listen with bated breath, straining toward her, anxious.

Her brother Andrew was part of the search party. By following beaver dams, they came upon signs of George's earlier presence. Recently broken ice that had frozen over again with slivers like shards of broken glass pointing to the sky. Snow melted from the heat of a fire. Based on the clues, George had been able to check all his traps. Then, all of a sudden, his snowshoe tracks vanished. In that spot, the spruce were twisted, and birch and aspen branches had been broken or torn from their trunks. As though a giant had shaken the trees with his huge hands, mangling them, tugging on their limbs....

Overcome with fear, the men retraced their steps as quickly as they could.

Koukoum pauses and takes a sip of tea. In a frightened, subdued voice, Maikanshish asks feebly, "Koukoum, do you think it was *Koukoujdi* the ogre who took Noumoushom George?"

Grandmother Who Wears Glasses laughs heartily to reassure him. "What do you think, Maikanshish?"

We all cry, "Oh! Oh! It must be the *Koukoudji! Koukoudji* ate our Noumoushoum. Yes, it's him!"

We shout out all kinds of theories till Maman pipes up, "Some claim he was taken by aliens from outer space." She tells her aunt about Josep's books that speak of flying saucers encountered by pilots in mid-air, of abductions, and the traces left of their passing such as twisted, broken trees. "Josep says they're nothing but tall tales, but then again, he says Miste Man'tou is only another superstition, too."

Our mother looks angry. However, Koukoum Who Is Black looks worried. The story told in books of flying saucers troubles her. She asks Maman if any witnesses saw these beings, the aliens.

"According to Josep, they look like bug-eyed grey or green grasshoppers. And not a single whisker or hair."

Reassured, Koukoum bursts into laughter. "*Iskwe*, your husband's pulling your leg! Grasshoppers in space! For a second, I thought our Great Fathers from the Wolf Star had returned to earth."

She laughs so hard our mother takes offense.

5

GEORGE
AUGUST 2004

ONCE AGAIN, the road winds on, this time without ki-lometre after kilometre of poles strung with wire. The sun is still shining. The extent of this uninhabited landscape of rocks, lichen, and burnt pine is mesmerizing. Nothing but the occasional car. The two of us silent, lost in thought, both remembering our trip to the Waskaganish museum while my cousin's revelations about his grandfather George trouble me.

Ahead of us, the road carved between two walls of stone climbs a hill. There's a vehicle driving on the shoulder. On its roof, a big handwritten sign reads: Save the Rupert River. To the left of the car a man in a blue tracksuit walks. He's from hereabouts. Alone but for the person at the wheel, perhaps his spouse, who keeps pace, he marches on, head down, eyes glued to the ground, shoulders tense with fatigue or anger. Daniel honks in support. Without looking up from the pavement, the man raises an arm, fist clenched.

We eat on the banks of the Rupert River. Its turbulent waters crash against the riverbed's massive rocks that have blocked the river's forward motion for centuries. That power soon to be tamed, harnessed, converted into comfort for people's homes.

At the intersection for Nemaska, the gauge shows we need more gas. I don't want to run any risks. We'll head straight for the next truck stop. And visit my great-aunt Caroline in Nemaska on our way back.

A dream. A man snowshoeing. He's having a rough go of it. Not because of the crusted snow, but because of the condition he's in. Day is drawing to an end. It's an unusual dream, as though confused with reality. Suddenly, I'm the man. I'm aching and afraid, my fear tinged with panic. I feel hunted. My skin bristles with pain. An animal's fangs lodge in my right leg and drag me down. I cry out in my sleep. Daniel shakes me awake. I sit up abruptly and take in my surroundings. We're in the tent; tears of relief and sorrow trickle from my eyes.

Daniel listens to me in the dark of night....

While the American, Tom, kept Daniel spellbound with tales from his well-stocked library on the history of the Hudson's Bay Company, my second cousin Stanley continued to share details with me about his grandfather George's disappearance. He dug through maps of Cree territory, unfurled an old map with great care and laid it out on the huge table that sat imposingly in the middle of the room. He pointed at one section circled in red. "Those are George's trapping grounds," he said.

Thinking out loud, I asked, "Where on earth could his body be in all that?"

"Ah-ha! What you don't know is that bones were found..."

With rising excitement, my breathing quickened. "Tell me, Stanley, I didn't know Great-Uncle was found!"

One day in the spring of 1970, during a dig, white prospectors looking for ore unearthed some bones. With surprise tinged with horror, they realized they had come upon a human foot and tibia. The rest of the body was missing. They reported their discovery to authorities, who had the bones analyzed to determine the deceased's age and gender. Since George's family had reported him missing in 1953 and the bones were those of a man of his age, his remains were handed over to the family. Strangely, however, those bones lay far from George's territory. In vain, people from his clan excavated the soil around where the discovery had been made, but the rest of his skeleton never surfaced.

Daniel says nothing. At one point, I think he's fallen asleep, but his hand comes to rest on my belly. A tender, comforting gesture.

"That's not all," I say. "Stanley mentioned fang marks on the bones. Daniel, my great-uncle was devoured, either alive or dead, most likely by a pack of starving wolves. I remember Koukoum Ka Wapka Oot talking about a period of famine. If there wasn't enough game for humans, there wouldn't have been enough for wolves either...."

I can picture the scene. Once again, I feel rising terror. This has got to stop. I fear for my sanity now that this is no longer a dream. It comes to me that George must have run on and on, fleeing the predators, losing his bearings and his last shred of courage.

"My dreams," I say, "My latest dreams warned me. George hasn't left. His spirit is still roaming there, he's begging for help! I have to find a way to appease his spirit."

Like the sudden lull after a storm, a stillness enters my belly and heart. I will be the instrument; I will follow the signs and we will see.

Accustomed to the odd phenomena that punctuate our life *à deux*, Daniel says in a sleepy voice, "Sweetheart, just say the word and off we'll go." After a few minutes, his regular breathing tells me he's fallen asleep.

I stare at the stars through our tent's mosquito netting, my mind churning with thoughts, memories, impressions. In memory, I follow scents, colours, and emotions, diffuse but so real. For instance, of all the adults who held me as a child, the strong odour that emanated only from my father's underarms. One my mother called his "white man scent...." People from our clan smelled of resin, smoked or roasted meat. Although his particular smell was overpowering, I grew to find it reassuring over the days during which happiness fled the family, and my father would gather me in his arms to keep my nightmares at bay.

Tonight, one impression in particular makes its way into my feverish mind. Difficult to grasp because it doesn't involve physical touch. I recognize my mother's, my grandmother's hands. My adoptive grandfather has gotten into the habit of shaking me, whether or not I'm crying. It's like a nervous tic, an inability to rock a child. As for the young girls in our clan, I soon lose patience with them too, feeling unsafe given the way they handle me. I cry, calling my mother to the rescue.

One day after being treated like a living doll all day, back home again, I crawl into a square of sunlight beneath the window. There I curl into a ball and fall fast asleep. Exhausted. It's then that the diffuse feeling rises, like a tenuous breath, but of total serenity and implicit trust in the person who discovers and gathers up the baby lying on the floor. His emotion, a blend of tenderness and infinite compassion, reaches my unconscious. Great-Uncle George. And his pact with me: the offer of gentle, comforting love that sees nothing but the human being hidden inside my tiny body.

The recollection of my great-uncle's presence brings me peace. Unhampered by the years or his death, I can feel the warmth of his affection and I slip into a deep sleep.

6

MATHEW AND MARY
JULY 1961

AFTER THE DEPARTURE of our grandmother Ka Wapka Oot, Maman packs up food and belongings enough for a week. July is scorching and hard to bear. The lack of sleep makes the boys turbulent and their scuffles have gotten the better of our mother's patience. We will travel to the tip of Shabogama Lake and camp on a beach of sand and wind. Our father will ferry us there in the barge he ended up building with the help of our neighbour, Mr. Plamondon. The barge makes it possible for us to travel together as a family. Papa will come for us after his week at work. He'll sleep with us tonight and leave early tomorrow.

Excited at the prospect of swimming in the lake and racing along the shore, the children help as best they can to ready our departure. Makwashish loads onto the boat the simple fishing rods my father makes to amuse his sons. At the age of three, Makwashish still inhabits the fantasy world of childhood. He tells Maman he'll keep us supplied with fish during our stay. Just in case, Maman brings her fishing net and the wooden floats she nearly forgot, and gently strokes my little brother's thick head of hair. Our family outings are true adventures. Already the breeze created by our motor-propelled speed cools us down. Our baby Sibi, swaddled to her underarms in the *tikinigan*, claps to show her pleasure. Her wooden cradleboard keeps her upright, propped against the side of the barge. She is my first sister. The sister I've longed for, for years.

We make shore after several hours on the water. The canoe we've towed behind will help us haul in the net. I unpack the prospector's tent on the spot Maman has chosen while my father and Jimmy look for a few small straight trees to cut down for the frame. The children squawk like a flight of birds in spring, splashing each other with cold water. Once our camp is set up, the big kids will go swimming. Our parents deploy the fishing net at the mouth of a river. Jimmy and I gather dead branches to cook our next meal with. We find dead trees to be felled over the coming days. Jimmy sets a brass snare on a trail well travelled by hare.

Maman never goes in swimming. She finds a flat rock to sit on, moistens a cloth, rubs in some soap and washes her body. Then she wades into the water up to her belly to rinse off. She's never completely naked; a skirt hides her crotch and buttocks. She does, however, bare her breasts, generous now after successive pregnancies. She nurses each of her babies until the next one's arrival.

Papa plays at picking up his sons and throwing them as far as he can into the lake. Careful with Maikanshish and Makwashish too, still little, he swings Demsy and Philou wildly. They scream, torn between pleasure and fear. Our mother cautions him to go easy. The game invariably ends in tears; one swallows a mouthful of water or the other collides with his brother in mid-air. I know my father's medicine and am careful to stay well back.

Not that I get off any more lightly when my turn comes. Today, my father plans to teach me how get back in the canoe if necessary. We never wear life jackets, they're not yet mandatory. He'd rather we know how to swim and climb back into the boat. So as not to make it any easier for me, he doesn't say a word—just sits in the middle of the canoe, keeping it steady with one of the paddles. In silence. For the longest time, I try to figure out how to climb in without tipping out my father, who's having a grand old time. I'm getting tired. Finally, my mother calls from shore, "Try from the end, my girl!"

My father was a taskmaster. Orphaned at a young age, his grandmother didn't spare the rod raising him. The way he brought us up was affected by what he'd experienced. He never thrashed us with an object, his broad hands were enough. But since his method never led to the desired result, he stopped using force after Maikanshish was born. Maikanshish was a good, calm boy who walked and talked at a very young age. Perhaps Papa realized that the little one had command of his world and held a poor view of his father, the grown-up. Our mother protected us as much as she could from our father's harsh ways. In her culture, children weren't punished.

Papa's absence allowed for a different family dynamic. We felt at ease, like soldiers out of sight of their general.

We've been at the beach for two days now. The good weather holds. The boys break trail through the woods tracking imaginary animals. Jimmy and I sit in the tent with Maman. Sibi lies under a light cotton sheet, fast asleep. From where we're positioned, we can keep an eye on our brothers. We don't often have an opportunity to speak to our mother; the boys demand all our attention.

I want to know the truth about her uncle George and his disappearance in the forest. His story fascinates me. At eleven, I no longer believe in Koukoum Who Is Black's ogres, or in Maman's aliens. Maman turns my question over in her mind, then responds. "Actually, I don't know. What saddens me is imagining his spirit roaming lost through the forest. No ceremony to guide him to Miste Man'tou.... It happened eight years ago already. The year Josep and I stopped travelling to the territory with the family. Back when we used to go, George never went out hunting alone, Josep was always with him."

Maman's mention of the Great Spirit has touched me; a secret cord vibrates deep inside. I don't understand what's just happened. I feel shaken and what seems like a thousand drums resound in my chest. My mother's voice comes to me from a great distance. "On my mother's side, strange things have happened in our family. Don't mention it to your brothers, they're too young. They wouldn't understand."

I listen, once again all ears. I love hearing real stories.

"When Koukoum Ka Wapka Oot mentioned that grand-father Mathew and my grandmother Mary were separated, the separation actually came about because Mathew spent five years in prison. For having got one of his own daughters with child...."

I catch my breath. What a hard thing to get my head around. How can a man be in love with his own daughter? Maman tells me that love has nothing to do with it; men ruin girls for their own gratification. For themselves. For their own pleasure. I glance over at my brother. Flustered, Jimmy looks away.

My mother tells us that, being ill, her grandmother Mary no longer took her husband into her bed. Her fifteen-year-old daughter Judy ran the household. Some gossips said she took her role as her mother's stand-in too seriously. The truth is her father raped her. When her pregnancy began to show, that truth became glaringly obvious to her mother, her brothers, and her sisters. They lived alone on their trapping grounds. Mary knew the fire in her husband's belly. Judy gave birth to a girl in disgrace and died soon after. Her brothers dug her grave, seething with rage. Mary looked after the frail baby who wasted away till she too followed her young mother to the other side. Her uncles laid her in a hollow they dug next to Judy's grave.

The story reached the ears of the RCMP and officers were sent to arrest Mathew. For incest, a crime punishable by law. Mathew confessed and was sentenced to five years in prison. Rumour reached the Company's trading posts that federal prison authorities were unable to keep Mathew under lock and key. It was said that the door would automatically unlock for him. They moved him to another cell. After a number of failed attempts, they hired Mathew as a janitor. According to Maman, he developed his uncanny gift from being a free man who was simply incapable of living in a cage.... With his wages, Mathew bought himself a canoe, a tent, and traps, and paddled from Cochrane, Ontario, to his territory in north-western Quebec.

Upon his return, he spoke a new language—English. Fearful, his family refused to open the tent flaps to him. They were afraid of this new man capable of works of wonder and evil. He was thought to be a trickster. But all Noumoushoum Mathew wanted was to live in the forest as he had done before. He pitched his tent close to his wife's camp so his sons could see and monitor him. He made no attempt to return to the clan. Several weeks later, his children began to pay him visits. After a few months, Abel, the eldest, counselled his mother to welcome her husband back into her tent. Grandmother Mary says she felt "unmarried" from Mathew, not only because of the rape and death of her daughter, but because of his lengthy absence as well. Abel offered to re-unite them during a traditional ceremony. Eventually, Mary agreed. The following year our grandmother Louisa was born, then George.... Mathew proved himself to be a good father and good husband to Koukoum Mary.

7

SMALL
AUGUST 2004

'

T HE CHIRPING of both children and birds wakes me from
the sleep I've lingered in for some time now, a prisoner to
the sleeping bag's warmth. Daniel is gone. I crawl out of the
tent, pleasantly drowsy still, my eyelids heavy. My husband
sits at the picnic table reading a novel. Our neighbours at the
next campsite, a man and his two children, are busy making
breakfast. I catch a whiff of pancakes and bliss. Daniel smiles.
"Hello, sleepyhead. Like some coffee?"

There are occasional moments of pure joy....

Carrying fishing rods, the man and his children climb into
a small motorboat. Once they've sped off, I spread my sacred
objects out on the shore. Facing east, accompanied by my rattle,
I chant a song to the earth, the water, the sun, the wind. I give
thanks. Again and again. Thank you, Life. My body expands
to vast proportions. I'm inhabited by the elements dancing in
a white light intersected by colourful flashes. I see the earth
far below and deep inside me. I am. I exist. I dance with my
brothers the animals, the plants, the stones, the Spirit of all
creation. I chant because, within me, surrounding me, my
Cree ancestors are also dancing. They will come to the rescue
of George's spirit.

Emerging from my meditation, my eyes meet Daniel's emotional gaze. He gives himself a shake. Soon we'll be off.

A friend suggested we visit the village of Wemindji for its
location and friendly inhabitants. We arrive well before lunch.

Its houses, built on sand, look unlived in. We leave our car on the huge beach that surrounds the community. I take off my sandals to feel fine sand gently massaging the soles of my feet.

Old Factory ... the name keeps running through my mind like one of Koukoum Kawap Ka Oot's tales. She told us of gatherings of our people, of clan reunions to share the happenings of the winter just past, and for match-making. From behind her hand, she giggled, remembering trysts with her Noah. Because of her advanced age, it was hard for me to imagine her young and burning with passion. Yet she flew with a wild goose's grace to the man who would become her husband.

In the rustling of leaves, I hear palaver's echo during *moukoushans,* the voices of grandparents telling tales, the excitement of young people sharing moments of pleasure. Wind gallops over the dunes and its turbulent, unbridled cavalcade drives away the mosquitoes bent on tormenting us. The location is magnificent. Did Koukoum Louisa and Noumoushoum George run and play behind their elders' back on the distant islands across the way? And Louisa, adolescent, was it here by the river that she smiled shyly at good-looking John Peesum Mapio for the first time?

Wooden picnic tables surround a tipi. A murmur rises from the tent, women's laughter. Tactfully, we give it a wide berth. Having noticed a restaurant on our arrival, we decide to head there for coffee to meet the locals and take Wemindji's pulse. I'd swear the town's whole population is seated within its walls smelling of fried eggs, toast, and sizzling bacon. We make our way to an empty table in the middle of the room, brushing past chairs occupied by happy, chattering Cree. Daniel notices several young white girls and a man seated. They're speaking in French.

We sit there for quite some time without being waited on. Strangely, the servers seem to be ignoring us. Deliberately looking anywhere else, but at us. We had more or less the same experience in Waskaganish at the inn. We were hoping to order dinner, but for some reason the staff thought we were invisible.

This morning I finally grasp the principle. It's a self-serve restaurant. We almost forget to pay for our coffee on the way out. The owner takes our word for it, "Just a coffee? It's my treat! Have a good day!" His eyes sparkle with the pleasure of hosting people in his restaurant.

As we make our way back to our car, I remember the caribou-hide moccasins I've been wanting to find. A white man and a Cree man are busy talking in the middle of the path under the shade of jack pines. I ask the Indigenous fellow whether the village has a handicraft shop. He responds with a question of his own. "D'you speak Cree? What's your name? Mine's Small!" He gives my hand a vigorous shake.

"Capississit, egoudeh haw? N'wakoumacht' nedeh Waswanipitch' Ka out'chee daw...."

Surprised and somewhat embarrassed, Mr. Small replies, "Actually, my real name is Capississit."

Mr. Small, like others before him, changed his Indigenous name to the European equivalent. It turns out he's related to me through my great-aunt Maria Peesum Mapio, who married a Capississit, He Who Is Small, from Waswanipi.

We talk about cousins we have in common including Emily, a childhood friend. He remembers his great-uncle John and his wife Louisa, my grandparents. Through him, I learn that my grandfather, a tuberculosis carrier, died a few short years after marrying Louisa, leaving her with two young children, their youngest Maggy having died at birth. So Koukoum's life had been riddled with sadness and loss.

8

LOUISA
JULY 1962

W E HAVEN'T LIVED near the Pointe-aux-Vents camp for
five years now. For a reasonable sum, my father bought a
partial plot of land with a cove on one side and a creek leading
to the river. Koukoum Louisa and the members of her family
took over our old cabin after we moved out. Memories come
back to me. Today my thoughts have turned to my grandmother
because I miss her. Maman's gone, who knows where.... My
hands are deep in the water I had to haul up the hill before I
could do the laundry. My brothers' mud-spattered clothes will
dry in today's sun and wind.

Born of Louisa's marriage to Samuel, an Algonquin, my uncle Jerry, only a few years older than my brother Jimmy, had
entered adulthood. Maman told us that, following his father's
example, he was unkind to Koukoum. Sometimes grandmother
Louisa showed up alone at our last house by way of the new
trail, longer by two kilometres. Her face sported bruises. Without saying a word, Maman would serve her a meal. We could
sense that a disaster had taken place. I stood nearby, racked
by a new-to-me sorrow. At six years old, I was helpless in the
face of her misfortune and hunger.

That summer, I sometimes followed my brother and his
new friends, our neighbours' sons, to the public dump. The
boys played with primitive slingshots, aiming at crows and
seagulls. Particularly good at it, Jimmy wanted to impress
his friends. One day, someone else had gotten there first. We

saw the crouching silhouette of a woman in a red-and-green plaid dress, her back turned to us. A huge wave of sadness and dreadful shame flooded over me. Grandmother Louisa sat wolfing down whatever meat she could find on a chicken carcass that must have come from some restaurant kitchen in the village. Ever thoughtful, she hadn't wanted to disturb our family by turning up to eat at our place. Her husband spent their meagre funds on alcohol.

Our neighbours, not knowing she was our grandmother but being well brought-up children, averted their gaze, as though looking for potential winged victims. Jimmy and I were dumbfounded. After a quick glance in our direction, Koukoum pretended she was on the lookout for things that could still be of use. She slowly walked away, as though she hadn't noticed our presence. She spared us any embarrassment in front of our friends by pretending she was in total control. A ball of acid formed in my belly and bile rose in my throat. I vomited.

Koukoum rushed over and wiped my lips with a cloth she pulled from the sleeve of her dress. In silence, our eyes locked. The boys, curious, surrounded us. Pulling myself to my full height, smaller than them all, I said in Cree, *"Ni n'koukoum!"* pointing at myself then my grandmother. I didn't speak French yet. Jimmy translated for me.

Back home, I asked my mother if Koukoum could live with us. We could protect her from her husband's and son's fists the way we used to…. That time Maman had tears in her eyes.

From then on, instead of following the boys, I took the trail along the river to Koukoum's carrying a hide bag full of fruit and a tin of food. Often I'd return with the bag still full; if my grandmother was away, I didn't want anyone else to eat my reserves. One day, however, Koukoum opened the door. Alone as usual, she took the canned meat and bananas with a distracted air, saying, *"Migwech't, Tititetch'. K'teemyeteem n'gooshish…."* Thank you, Little Little One, my son will be very happy….

I don't remember what came next. A wave of sadness, I think, flooding a little girl's heart as she ran down a trail obstructed by roots like the small spruces' big toes that kept tripping her, blinded as she was.

Late that fall, Koukoum, who would occasionally come and stay with us for a few days, tells us she doesn't feel well. My father takes her to see the village doctor. Despite our concern, we all manage to laugh when she gets stuck in the rocking chair too narrow for her bottom. Maman holds onto the chair as Papa helps her out. She chuckles softly. Koukoum has to go to the Amos hospital. Her body, too often deprived of nourishment and proper care, loses its grip on a love for life. She gestures vacantly now as though her spirit were travelling elsewhere.

We receive letters from the hospital that only Maman can read. She writes to Koukoum in Cree syllabics, never forgetting to slip a stamp inside her return envelope. Our grandmother writes that she is well-looked after and well-fed despite her lack of appetite, that she's resting, that she's keeping warm. Convinced she'll be back soon, my worries vanish.

But Koukoum doesn't return.

Winter marches on. Slow. Long. Grey. Only the birth of a little brother in November breaks up the days' unchanging nature. Over Easter, Maman dresses us in our finest. The promise of spring is in the air. We're to take the train to visit Koukoum. We're excited to be travelling for the first time on the smoke-belching engine. For once we're calm, given over to the overwhelming joy of seeing our grandmother again. We miss her so much!

She greets us sitting up in bed under white sheets. She smiles. My brothers scatter around her, planting snot-nosed kisses on her. She welcomes their affection, her shoulders shaking in silent laughter. It's my turn to kiss her cheek. Koukoum smells of soap. A long braid of her luxuriant hair, as black as ever, crowns her head.

She is beautiful, looks at peace, happy even. We talk to her for hours as we wait for the next train home. She holds her newest grandson in her arms until it's time for us to leave. At the station, Maman treats us to hot dogs to reward us for our good behaviour. Our happiness is complete.

Our parents hide the real state of Koukoum's health from us. It does feel like she's spent a long time in hospital, but she's doing so much better....

It was after this visit to see our grandmother that a well-dressed man sporting a tie drove up to the house. He brought a briefcase full of papers with him. He tried to communicate with Maman, but other than Jimmy who knew a bit of French, no one could answer him in our father's absence. The man gestured toward Jimmy and me with his free hand. One word worried us because we'd often heard it used by our neighbour friends—school. In fact, neither Jimmy or I went to school, unlike the others who headed off to residential school or the village school in the red-and-white milk truck.

The man left papers on the table for our father. Back from work, Papa read the documents that saddened him. He told Maman they had to add us to the list of schoolchildren on the concession road. I was in turmoil hearing Papa say, "The law gives us no choice!" Should we be happy that at least Jimmy had been able to stay with us until he was ten? Jimmy wasn't just my big brother, he'd been my only friend since our move. The thought of not seeing him for a whole ten months paralyzed me. My life was changing. At the age of seven, I saw my parents forced to send me to the village school come September on the red-and-white truck that smelled of cows and rancid milk.

The night before Jimmy left for residential school, I woke from a nightmare. I was crying so hard my parents knelt by my bed to comfort me.

Papa said, "You'll see, *Ikwesish,* you'll like school."

Maman said, "You'll come home every day after school."

Ashamed, despite my sadness, I didn't reveal the reason for my tears. I was losing my brother. My playmate.

One radiant October day, I come home from school wearing my blue uniform and white blouse, my bag slung across my shoulder, my lunch box in my hand. Maman smells of alcohol. She says, "Koukoum died this morning. Don't cry. Look, I'm not crying."

Then she heads for the path that leads to our old cabin where her stepfather and his half-sister Maryann must be waiting for her return with their gallon of cheap St-Georges wine. I collapse onto my parents' queen bed, my face buried in the duckdown quilt, my bag and lunch box at the end of my splayed arms. I sink into a deep, dark hole, gasping for air.

Later, once supper's over, Papa puts us in the canoe, the youngest crouched between his legs. Maikanshish is almost eleven months old. No one says a word. We land below the hill on which our abandoned cabin stands. I hear Koukoum's husband wailing in a slurred voice, a few English words mixed in with the Algonquin.

Papa says, "Look after your little brothers, I'll be right back." He jumps nimbly from the boat and climbs easily and quickly in the direction of the voice.

Shortly afterwards, we see our father reappear, profiled against the evening sky. He peers over our mother in his arms, careful to keep his footing on the clay slope as he carries her down. He lays Maman on the bottom of the canoe, gently, making sure not to bump her against anything. His face grimaces with the strain and his eyes, behind their round glasses, speak of untold hurt. Immense worry invades my chest. Grim, raw, rough. It sinks its claws into my belly and shakes me sick.

9

CHEVALIER
AUGUST 2004

W E LEAVE WEMINDJI. At the turn-off for the James Bay road, we stop for lunch at a picnic table. En route, we passed several cars going the other way, including Tom's, the genealogist from the Waskaganish museum. He neither saw nor recognized us. What's going on in Wemindji?

A van stops as we're getting lunch ready. Several Cree climb down and head for the outhouses. I call to one of the young women as she walks by, "Is there something special on in Wemindji today?"

It turns out that an annual gathering of the communities is about to take place, hosted by Wemindji. Damn! My disappointment doesn't go unnoticed by Daniel. He stirs the pasta sauce. Without saying a word, he waits to see what I'll do. There's something I need to pick up at the drugstore, plus we don't have enough fresh fruit. We need a hot shower. Our plan was to go to Radisson to run our errands. Neither of us can make up our mind. A coin toss will make the decision for us. Heads, we retrace our steps, tails we keep going. Tails! Oh well, too bad!

A few indomitable Québécois have put down roots in Radisson. I'm surprised to see rose bushes blooming at this latitude. In front of the hotel lobby, I notice beds of blue flowers—monk's hood! We walk into a craft store that has quite the collection: African masks, Inuit sculptures, jewellery, smoked caribou-hide mitts and moccasins. But none in the size

I'm looking for. We find a display featuring regional products. We choose some caribou pâté and a large trout that I'll serve with rice and chanterelles.

Our shopping over, we visit the campground. It has a self-service laundromat inside a long motor home. So we'll camp here. Since it's still early afternoon, we stroll down Radisson's sidewalks. A warm breeze keeps the mosquitoes at bay. I consider the human capacity to adapt to any environment. I'm not surprised the Cree love this land, its landscape is in their blood and soul. But even European descendants have grown so attached that they don't want to leave once the power stations are built! They're like their rosebushes, their monk's hood growing in a hostile climate, whose flowers boldly emerge with the first warm rays of a short summer season. Stubborn.

The next day, we head for Chisasibi. It's a Sunday so we take our time driving, sure there won't be much going on in the morning. Halfway there, we're stopped by a barrier. The guard, a young Cree man, jots down our licence plate number, our names and addresses. He tells us the Cree are strictly prohibited from bringing alcohol into the community. A decision made by the band council after too many accidents and suicides caused by substance use. Alcohol, a poison to the system, does not alleviate the community's suffering.

We drive slowly through quiet streets. We note with interest a pretty white and blue chapel surrounded by greenery. Originally built by Catholic missionaries offshore, on the island where the Cree used to live, it was towed on a huge raft and transplanted to the new village of Chisasibi.

We park our car in the chapel's yard. There's more going on here. A game played by three girls attracts our attention. Poorly shod, one even in high heels, they run down the gravel road ahead of moving cars. They laugh hysterically, excited by the danger. Drivers come to a full stop, afraid they'll hit the girls as they drive by. I lose my desire to give them a scolding when one of the girls falls, bloodying her knees and the palms of her hands. She shrieks in pain while her friends help her to her feet. The dangerous game is over and we can breathe again.

The bustle across from the chapel awakens our curiosity. Dozens of cars are busy parking around a brick building. A Pentecostal temple. In no time, a hundred or so cars have gathered there; not one of them comes our way. Then a young woman, either Japanese or Chinese, walks over and climbs the steps to the chapel. We greet her. Daniel asks if we can visit the inside of the church. "Yes, sure," she says in English.

We aren't alone. Four men are busy discussing the ceremony they're about to perform. A Catholic priest is no longer available at all times, so they pray without benefit of the sacrament of the Eucharist. Feeling somewhat uncomfortable since I'm no longer a follower of Christian religions, I wander off to look at the decor and photographs on the walls.

Daniel discusses the chapel's history with a tall, athletic-looking, redheaded man. The conversation turns to research being done on a shipwrecked merchant ship that hit the rocky coast during a big storm in the nineteenth century. It belonged to the French firm Révillon, bent on competing with the Hudson's Bay Company in the fur trade. After the shipwreck, the sailors transferred the bundles of merchandise onto lifeboats and headed for an island. Soon after, the Cree came into contact with them. Most of the French sailors decided to return south in their flimsy boats. Only Martin Chevalier stayed behind on the island to watch over the merchandise.

He offset his solitude by taking a Cree wife, who gave him two children, a boy and a girl. His daughter died at a young age in a horrific accident. She succumbed to burns when a pail of scalding water fell onto her. It's said that Chevalier nearly lost his mind and, to survive, left his family behind to push further west where he opened his trading posts for the Révillon company.

However, the son left behind with his mother lived such a long life that he produced numerous descendants. That is why there are still Cree today who bear the name Chevalier, some of whom work in retail.

We make for the Chez Pash snack bar for hamburgers and fries. Just this once. I speak to the waiter in Cree. He goes back behind the counter, tells the cook I don't have an accent, and I hear them laughing. Afterward, they couldn't have been nicer. As we take our seats, two Québécois walk into the restaurant. They head in our direction and ask to share our table. We nod.

They talk about contracts they're working on, slowly, at the Cree pace. I expect to hear them pass judgment on the nonchalant work attitude, but they both appreciate the extra time it gives them to go fishing. We hit it off right then and there.

A little girl comes up and points at my piece of cake. She sits on my lap, determined to eat my dessert. I tease her, *"Pschii ... Nin' nehe n'midjim!"* She grimaces and crosses her arms.

Her mother calls her over and the little girl leaves with a smile. Transfixed, the two Québécois stare at me. My métissage suddenly sinks in. "Kinda thought so!" says the younger one.

We can't go any farther; the road ends at Chisasibi. If we drive fast, we could make it back to Nemaska. Not wild about that idea, we backtrack aimlessly instead. Late that afternoon, we see a sign for a campground at Mirrabelli Lake by the road to Eastmain. For some reason, the Eastmain village is of no interest to us.

Onsite, we come across the family man and his pancake-loving children. They wave at us from a distance. A blustering wind makes pitching our tent a challenge. As usual, we anchor it in place with stones. Late that evening, the wind dies down and we're able to light a campfire beneath the stars. Warm and cosy, wrapped in blankets, Daniel and I meditate by the flames. Above us, the dark sky autographed by shooting stars fills us with wonder. It's the season for Perseid meteor showers. Lying on my back gazing into infinity, I thank Creation for such majesty.

The night carries me off again into the country of the invisible, of dreams. From a valley through which a quiet river runs, I look on a mountain. A red-antlered caribou steps out from between the rocks and trees, its eyes on me. I make my way to the river and suddenly hear the muffled sound of an entire herd's hooves on the opposite shore. The red-antlered male stands at the head of his harem. A stranger walks over to me and says, "Go see Humbert...." The stranger is so tall I have to crane my neck back to see him. "I have two territorial poles to carve first." The man walks away.

The next day at breakfast, I tell David about my dream. The lack of clarity in dreams frustrates me. Why not put things simply? My husband's humorous retort, "That's exactly why, you'd think it was too simple." Suddenly, my heartbeat speeds up. That name, Humbert, so strange, must have a tie to Uncle George—that's what he'd called me in a recent dream. At the Waskaganish Inn!

10

DAISY

JULY 1962

W E'RE WALKING down the trail to the village. It's a struggle for Maman to push the baby carriage over the stones. We're off to visit our family back at their summer camp. Since Koukoum Louisa's death, no one has lived in our old cabin, now overgrown with weeds. The spot where the tents are pitched advances onto the river. At Pointe-aux-Vents, we use a stand of tall birch trees as our perch. From there, we spy on the *Mistikouji,* whose houses are scattered along the opposite bank. There's a sawmill whose resiny scent wafts our way. A memory lingers—my father jumping from one log to the next armed with a pole. Maman confirms that he did work for a few weeks as a log driver before finding his current job. I tell Maman she didn't like to see Papa working on the logs. She looks at me in astonishment. "You're right, it had me worried. How do you know that? You were barely three."

We enter the space opening onto wind and water. Our cousins greet us warmly. A surprise awaits our mother. Allaisy announces that Daisy, Uncle George's eldest daughter, is sharing her tent. Right away, Maman wants to see this cousin for whom she has a soft spot. With an embarrassed laugh, Allaisy gestures to the point along the river. She says, "She's fishing for critters...."

My cousins motion for me to run with them to join Daisy. From the point, I see a young woman, her legs exposed to mid-thigh. With her skirt tied in a big knot in front, she carries a pail and is wading slowly through the water, staring into the depths. She stays motionless for a good while, then plunges her bare arm into the water to grab hold of something. A singular spectacle. Cree women are invariably modest in public and her daring astonishes me. My cousins make fun of my astonishment. Daisy is fishing for freshwater mussels. Another singularity. No Cree eats those disgusting, slobbering things! My friends shout, "Daisy, there's someone here to see you!"

She turns to us and, from a distance, I see her broad smile opening over white teeth. She calls, *"Tititech'! Nash weskit shash ti wapmin'din'!"* Little Little One! I haven't seen you for so long! She adds, "You've gotten so big!"

I have no memory of her.

Slowly she makes her way back to shore, feeling her way over the riverbed slippery with rocks. She hugs me to her. I feel a bit uncomfortable. I'm no longer used to gestures of affection, I'm too big now. When she sees my mother, she cries overjoyed, "Frances! Oh! Frances, my cousin, my beautiful cousin!"

Without a doubt, this cousin of Maman's is unlike all the others. She says what she thinks, doesn't hold back. I don't often hear compliments being voiced by other Cree, they generally come from my father and his people. Then she begins to speak. Without pause, without taking time to think. I listen, dumbfounded. She tells my mother how much she appreciated the residential school where she lived for years. The nuns who ran it, so kind and cultured, who taught her so much! Such a shame that Maman didn't have the same opportunity! But then she wouldn't have had such beautiful children, which is easily worth as much as an education, a love story crowned with marvelous angels.... She makes my head spin.

But I've finally met the cousin Maman envies for her ability to speak, read, and write in English. Koukoum Louisa wouldn't let my mother leave her side no matter how much she wanted to go to school. As a widow, my grandmother had to look after her young son Charley, and Maman helped her with the family's work. When Koukoum remarried, it was too late for

Maman to start school. Which has remained a constant source of frustration for Maman. Today she seems so happy to see Daisy that I banish those thoughts from my mind.

Behind my mother, good-looking Basile Gull eyes Daisy greedily. He's accompanied his aging parents, here for the summer for a religious ceremony celebrated by a Pentecostal preacher. Daisy says she works for the nuns now, that's why she doesn't come back to see the family. I can tell Basile has other plans for her that would mean she wouldn't return to Sault Ste. Marie. Marriages are often entered into when different clans camp together.

I'd already been the subject of dealings between Cree and Algonquin mothers looking for a future spouse for their sons, themselves barely older than me. I blushed at the women's efforts to size me up. Maman pointed out that since my father didn't follow the same customs, he wouldn't look favourably on such proposals. I could breathe again. And silently thank Papa for being my father!

Daisy did board that train going back south.

Two years later, Maman received a letter from Sault Ste. Marie written in English. Papa translated it.

Daisy announced that she'd stop in at the village during the time of the family reunion at the Pointe-aux-Vents camp. She asked if we could pick her up at the train station. Maman was delighted, thinking her cousin would spend some time with us at the house.

We are all at the station that morning: Jos, Allaisy, their children, Koukoum Ka Wapka Oot, the Roberts, cousin Emily and us. In those days, the train travelled by night. We're expecting to see a tired Daisy. Finally, the locomotive pulls in at the station. Travellers disembark, most looking exhausted. We search for Daisy among them. After the last passenger steps off, we see three nuns standing there facing us, immobile on the running board. Someone says, "Great Spirit alive, what on earth has she gone and done?"

Among the women, behind the brown and white veil encircling her forehead, each of us recognizes Daisy. I look at Maman. Her eyes mist over with a great sadness.

11

HUMBERT
AUGUST 2004

D ANIEL AGREES to double back to Waskaganish. Feeling sick, in part over the missed encounter with Great-Aunt Carolynn, I've also started to worry about the business around Uncle George's story. What if I've got it wrong? I can feel my parents arguing inside my head. Papa's voice calls it all superstitious nonsense, but my mother's urges me on. Daniel's is somewhere between the two. After all, it was his choice to follow me on this journey to my origins.

At Waskaganish, I ask my husband to stop at the craft store for the caribou moccasins I hope to find. An old man with wrinkled features sits in a chair outside the store. He's wearing tinted glasses and his hands lean on a cane carved from a curved piece of wood. I open the door only to meet the gaze of my cousin Stanley, as surprised to see me as I him. Leaning on the counter, he's busy talking to the salesclerk. He's happy to introduce me to the young woman, "Shirley, my wife...."

"What a coincidence!"

Those are Daniel's words as he too steps inside and catches sight of Stanley. My cousin laughs. Daniel takes in Shirley's beauty, admiring her auburn locks inherited from a Scottish grandmother. Her features—although freckled—and the colour of her skin are still typically Cree.

I ask Stanley if he'd have an hour to talk to me about his grandfather and if he could take me to the museum. He agrees. As we step outside, he touches the shoulder of the patriarch sitting by the door. Stanley wishes him a good day. We realize the man is blind. My cousin climbs into our car and we set out for the museum. The Elder turns his face in our direction.

I don't know how to explain my problem to Stanley. After all, he barely knows me. I decide to start at the beginning, telling him how our trapping grounds were divided among my parents, my grandparents, and his grandfather. And about the fleeting contact I'd had with the latter for a few years only during my childhood. Then I tell him about the dreams I've been having since my first visit to Waskaganish. Fascinated, Stanley says nothing. Trying not to let it show, he's still moved by the dream of a wolf attacking his grandfather. I'm reassured. He doesn't think I sound ridiculous. His emotion draws me closer to him.

Uncomfortable, Daniel hides behind a big book. Stanley locks his dark, intense gaze on me. "You have the gift," he says, "like a few other *Nede ni yu min,* now departed, although I've never seen a woman with it...."

To lighten the atmosphere, I tell him I may have inherited it from our great-grandfather Mathew, the unfit father who couldn't be kept behind bars, a traitor who kept his word.... Like every other Domind, Stanley knows our ancestor's story. It makes him laugh.

Following the thread of my dreams, I ask if he might know of someone whose first or last name is Humbert. As my words take me back to the land of dreams and the images linked to the name, Stanley just about topples over. "That man in tinted glasses sitting in front of my wife's store? His name is Johnny Humbert Mistanapeo!"

The shock has him speaking in Cree. I translate for Daniel, a lump in my throat. Silence descends. The dream has just penetrated reality. Mistanapeo means "The Great Man." Then my own voice pulls me from the dream, "Last night, the messenger spirit told me to find Humbert...."

Before we return to the shop, I want to ask my second cousin about a detail that slipped my mind during our previous visit.

I'd like to see on a map the exact location of George's old trapping and hunting grounds, and find out the name of the person who inherited them. From a large white metal filing cabinet, Stanley pulls out a map of north-western Quebec. He points at one spot with the tip of his pencil—Rupert River. He's ahead of me. "Cousin," he says, "if you go there, I want to come along!"

I don't know what's in store, but feel lucky knowing he'll be with me should I travel to his grandfather's territory. "We'll go if needed, Stanley, now that I think about it my most vivid dreams took place when we were camping between the Rupert and Eastmain rivers. Strange.... That's not that far from his grounds."

He adds, "We've got no time to lose, that land's soon to be flooded by Hydro-Québec's dams. The Rupert River is to be rerouted. Afterward, it may be too hard to navigate."

"When?" The question comes from Daniel.

"In November."

Part of my resolve collapses.

12

CLARENCE AND ANGÉLIQUE
MAY 1963

A KNOCK SOUNDS at the door. Because of the rain, we're stuck inside the walls of our home on this Saturday morning. Sprawled on our parents' bed, the boys look at pictures in a comic book. I'm doodling in a notebook on the kitchen table. Maman's making bannock. We all look up at the same time to see who's come calling. A beaming Billy Ottereyes makes a wry face behind the window, already anticipating the ribbing he'll give me about boys.

Of course, Billy too is one of Maman's second cousins. He's funny but teases me too much for my liking. His hatchet-carved features are surprising in their comical homeliness. Billy hasn't come alone this time.

My eyes light up in wonder and surprise at the sight of the young man standing behind our cousin's tall lanky frame. My mother's squeals of excitement barely register, nor does the coarse laughter coming from Billy, who's pleased at the surprise he's sprung on us. Holding my breath, all I hear is a name—Clarence…. Beauty personified. Light. Clarence. In the ensuing confusion, I manage to take another breath and regain some self-control. The boys surround the two men, bombarding them with questions. Billy always brings us mints during his annual visits. An impertinent Philou asks Clarence, "Where are you from? Are you Billy's son?"

"Yes and no," Clarence replies with a half-smile. He takes great pleasure in confounding Philou.

"That can't be!" my brother retorts. "Billy can't be your dad and not be your dad!"

The adults laugh and I just think my brother's a fool. I'm jealous of his ability to forge a bond with Clarence, who shoots me curious, interested glances. At twelve, I've begun to look like the teenager I'll soon be. Men's eyes disarming me of childhood innocence are proof of my nascent curves. I find it all quite angst-filled. Yet I've already blossomed in the silence of time's passing.

Clarence explains that Billy married his mother, who was widowed when he was two. He lives in Waswanipi and is seventeen. I do some quick mental math. Clarence is only a year older than Jimmy. More importantly, he's not a blood relative! As if reading my mind, Billy hits the bull's-eye with his question, "So, *Ishkwesh,* how do you like my Clarence?"

My face crimson, I'm prey to a distressing jumble of emotions. My mother comes to my rescue and tells Billy that's enough teasing. He stops when he sees my eyes fill with tears. He pats my hand, embarrassed at my reaction. Shame washes over me at the thought that Clarence has witnessed my confusion. My admission.

From then on, Clarence comes back to visit us on his own. He likes my mother's company and her sense of humour. I think he likes me, too. Alas, I already know this first love is hopeless. Maman warns Clarence how possessive my father is, watching me like a dog protecting its bone. She says, "Josep will never let an Eenou man marry his daughter."

This time, I wish my father was different. It feels like Maman uses Papa as a wall around me. She's constantly having to weave her way between the Cree culture and her husband's....

That summer, Koukoum Ka Wapka Oot tents with the family and the Algonquins at Pointe-Aux-Vents. She includes Clarence, her nephew Billy's adopted son. One Algonquin family is camping for the first time, the Wabanakis. There Clarence meets Angélique, a fetching young girl with burning wolf eyes.

Despite his seductive good looks, Clarence is intimidated by young women. All he can think of is to run to my mother to confide his feelings. I learn all about the unconscious cruelty of which a young lovestruck man is capable.

"Will she follow me to Waswanipi?"

Such is his dilemma. Maman warns him against the girl. "She has fits and falls to the ground drooling." Maman says she thinks the girl is crazy and scary.

I don't know if love alleviates Angélique's fits, but the fact is she doesn't have any that summer. Her parents feel she's too young at sixteen to wed, but perhaps the following year. They want to buy time to get used to the idea that she'll leave for another community, become part of another culture.

Since the spring, Papa's been digging out back of the house. Making a nuclear shelter. He works for the National Defence Department and knows that the Union of Soviet Socialist Republics and the United States of America are cooking up a cold war. He fears a bomb launched from northern Russian. We're all anxious, but try not to think about the possibility of a war of the titans that could annihilate us all like a swarm of mosquitoes.

Clarence comes over more often to talk to Maman. He's worried about his fiancée, who's distraught over the prospect of a bomb. She believes that white men will destroy earth. She often cries. Maman tries to put her young friend's mind at ease. She tells him, "You do know that her parents are cousins. It's not a good thing to fall in love and have children together when our fathers and mothers are almost brothers and sisters. It makes for fragile children and ... it's not an Eenou custom."

Over the weeks, I see Clarence's light slowly dim. I hate Angélique.

In late September, shortly before the hustle and bustle of departure for the hunting and trapping grounds, we visit our cousins in Pointe-Aux-Vents. Two police cars parked on the shoulder of the road in front of the trail leading to the camp alarm Maman, who urges us to hurry. No one comes to greet us as they usually do. Tents are empty. However, all the canoes are out on the water close to shore. Men stand using long poles to rake the riverbed. Women and children look on from the riverbank. The Wabanaki family members sit slumped on the ground, mute with sorrow, spent.

Koukoum Ka Wapka Oot walks over to my mother and whispers in her ear, "It's Angélique ... she's been missing since yesterday evening. We searched everywhere late into the night."

"And Clarence?" The question erupts from both my mother's lips and my own.

Koukoum wipes away a tear with her sleeve. "Poor boy, he got hold of some strong liquor and I don't know where he's hiding. He paid a cabdriver to buy that damn *skoude nabou* for him! That firewater...."

Eventually, Angélique's body rose to the surface. Her round belly attested to an early pregnancy. Too lovestruck, Clarence hadn't wanted to spend a year away from Angélique. The pregnancy forced her parents to bless their union as quickly as possible. Alas, the young woman's fragile mental state led her to end her days rather than continue to face her horrific fears and the choices of an adult life.

Clarence's light was extinguished. His handsome face folded in on its bitterness, his eyes reddened by each drunken binge.

Billy came to his rescue and dropped in on us one day with his stepson. He no longer laughed or teased me. My father came home from work. Seeing Billy and Clarence, he flew into a jealous rage and chased them out of our life. Yet they were the only ones who never asked my mother to buy liquor for them or pushed her to drink. My father dug a hole of solitude for us not unlike his nuclear shelter.

Still worried, Billy nevertheless returned to Waswanipi, leaving Clarence at the Pointe-Aux-Vents camp. A few days later in the dark of night, the train engineer didn't have time to brake when he caught sight too late of a body lying across the tracks. The firewagon cut Clarence in three. An empty bottle of St-George wine was found not far from his corpse.

13

MISTENAPEO

AUGUST 2004

THE OLD MAN in tinted glasses is no longer sitting in front of the store. Shirley tells her husband that Mistenapeo must be down by the river or at the inn since one of his granddaughters dropped by to take him for a walk. His daily exercise. I feel equal measures of urgency and restraint. Curiosity and a fear of the unknown and the invisible roil together in the pit of my stomach, making me feel slightly nauseous.

Stanley spots the Elder sitting on a bench behind the inn facing the Rupert River. My cousin heads in his direction. Daniel and I stand at a respectful distance, waiting to see what's to come. The two men exchange a few words, then Stanley returns.

"Humbert would like to meet you alone," he says, then turning to Daniel, "I'll treat you to a coffee if you like...."

I clutch my husband's arm. Seeing my gesture, Stanley gives me a gentle pat on the back. "Don't be afraid, cousin! Have faith, Mistenapeo is a wise man."

I slowly make my way over to him, fearful, full of doubt and apprehension. It's as though he's watching me from behind the shield of his glasses. A great kindness emanates from his features, lit by a reassuring smile. In a low, rasping voice, he invites me to sit next to him. Then, with his carved cane, he points at something above the river. *"Tshegon'ma t'wapten'nedeh?"*

Eagles! How ever did he see them? I screw up my courage and ask him to show me his eyes. *"N'kati wab'maouch'a ti stichuck'ch...?"*

He takes off his glasses and reveals eyes blank under a thick cloud of cataracts. They remind me of my father's eyes, turned a uniform grey by the same disease. Under his cap, Mistenapeo's straight hair falls to the nape of his neck, black and abundant. Even at an advanced age, unless they have some European ancestor, certain Crees' hair never turns white.

Gradually, calm returns to me. I feel both light and heavy at once. Mistenapeo breaks the silence with a teasing laugh, "I had trouble convincing you to come to me … had to appeal to the spirit of all the caribou in the land."

Caught off balance, my ears start ringing. *"T'schi na he?"*

My astonishment sparks his laughter, a thundering waterfall. Seeing his amusement, I too laugh. The atmosphere lightens, more conducive now to an exchange around the remarkable universe of the invisible. My rational mind strives to understand. Questions jostle in my brain, but I know enough to let Humbert proceed at his own pace. As though reading my mind, the old man speaks in his slow way, "A long time ago, when I was young, your great-uncle George and I were friends. The best of friends. His decision to marry a girl from Waswanipi separated us physically, but he always remained in my heart. He was a brother to me…. Before contact with the white world, our people often had the power to see visions. The descent into workaday values and alcohol abuse deadened that ability for most Eenouch. Add their religions to the mix…."

An awkward pause.

"When you were here last week, your dream tapped into a message sent to me by George's spirit. He put me in touch with you, but your Sherlock Holmes' mentality kept you from interpreting the dream properly."

I can't help but laugh at myself and at the idea that this man knows the Conan Doyle character. I share my thought with him.

"I loved watching Holmes' and his friend Dr. Watson's investigations on TV back when I could still see." This time, he speaks in English. I laugh even louder. If Daniel is watching from the inn, I wonder what he's thinking. I have trouble keeping my laughter in check, but Humbert doesn't seem offended, in fact he piles it on.

After he's cracked several more jokes, I ask a few questions that have been puzzling me. How did he manage to speak to me in a dream? Why me? What can I do for Uncle George?

Serious now, Mistenapeo answers. For as long as he can remember, he has practised shamanism, often repudiated by the pastors and priests who have followers among the Cree. His spirit travels to places simple mortals cannot reach. If George's spirit is calling to me, it's possible that I have "signed a spiritual contract" with him and that the time has come to honour it. Humbert says his friend's spirit can't leave the sphere of emotions, infused as it is with the horrendous fear that surrounded his death. His spirit stagnates waiting for an opening to the Light.

I'm in total science fiction territory. Another question, this one a bit more impatient, "But given your powers, can't you do that?"

Humbert Mistenapeo gropes for my hand, finds it, and gives a gentle squeeze. "*N'Danch, ka tchi kchi doden....*" My girl, you too can....

He says all shamans must test their gifts. That they are few and far between. That survivors like him will soon die and need to pass on their knowledge before the great departure. That humans both living and dead need help.

I'm dazed. It all seems more than a little complicated .

Humbert senses my resistance. "You're free," he tells me, "totally free to choose your path. No one can make you. The gift you possess belongs to no one, not even you. It belongs to the Great Mystery."

His words, like a warm shower to my soul, dilute the weight that has kept me glued to the ground and I feel propelled far away. From my vantage point, a huge flaming eagle circles earth. I'm barely breathing. A thousand drums sound in and around me. Then I see millions of caribou under whose hooves my heart trembles. My heart is Earth itself.

14

ANNA
NOVEMBER 2002

W E'RE LEAVING the church. Rain has fallen on the fresh snow. Today, we'll bury Sibi's body. In the church square, three Indigenous women, strangers, yet whose faces look familiar, hold their hands out to me. The eldest speaks in English, "I'm Anna, your mother's cousin and George's daughter. My sisters Sally and Sarah...."

On this day of deep suffering, their presence brings a gentle moment of respite. I hug them in turn. Anna takes my hand and tells me she used to babysit Jimmy and me the summer she spent with us before I was one. Her gaze is one of great affection. She looks like my mother and Koukoum Louisa. Now I recognize the girl we wondered about in the pictures Papa received five years ago from an old German photographer. It was in a photo album commenting on the life and traditions of the Cree living in the Pointe-Aux-Vents camp. For me, it was an unanticipated gift. Professional photographs showing my parents, Jimmy, grandmother Louisa, and me. And Anna. Snapshots of day-to-day life in the camp.

The anecdote surrounding the album sounds truly far-fetched. The photographer, passing through our village, was looking for someone to put him in contact with Indigenous peoples. He was sent to see my father, who agreed to act as his interpreter and middleman. In the course of their conversations, they discovered that they'd been on the same front in Germany during the final assault on the city of Berlin by

Allied forces. At the very same time, one on either side of the barricades, each shooting at the enemy. The German boy, seventeen, was part of the youth Waffen-SS sent under enemy fire as a last resort. The adults assigned to other fronts were losing the war.

Lost in my own thoughts, my own suffering, I forget to mention the album to Anna. Daniel urges me to tell her.

Looking up, I see my father propped up by my sisters Margaret and Élizabeth. He wears the mask of an old man defeated by sorrow. During a drunken binge fourteen years earlier, a man thrust a knife into Jimmy's chest, severing his aorta. Witnesses say that the man, jealous, meant to stab his wife, but my brother used his body as a shield to protect her. As the accidental victim of the man's murderous rage, had this been a way for Jimmy to put an end to his wretched existence?

Nine months later, it was Maman's turn to die, her liver ravaged by alcohol. The same firewater that has, without mercy, swept Sibi into its waters today. Alcohol's pull began for Maman after Koukoum Louisa's death and Jimmy's departure for residential school. She was able to keep her drinking somewhat under control for a few years, but after Sibi's birth, on school days, Maman would walk out of the house, abandoning the little ones once we'd left for school. The family suffered the aftershock of our mother's foundering because, under alcohol's sway, Maman became cruel, monstruous. Tyrannous....

I can't seem to cry. A lump as hard as rock blocks my throat. My voice like the trickle of a dried-out creek. My family and our guests make their way to their cars. We've provided for a funeral reception in a community hall. They are all there. Philou, trudging and grumbling like an angry bear. Demsy, despondent, eyes red from tears, lack of sleep, and alcohol. Maikan, impenetrable, held up by his partner. Makwa, grown so tall and thin, weeps uncontrollably between his wife and son. Then Édouard, my youngest brother, whose silent sorrow can be seen in his misty gaze. Élizabeth and Margaret accompany Papa to keep their minds occupied.

Anna and I continue our conversation over dinner. Among her memories of the family that she shares with me, I'm especially struck by the noble quality of my mother's being. Upon her death, other members of the extended clan also expressed the same respect for her. They've transferred to me, the eldest, the affection they had for her. Anna gives me her address and makes me promise to visit her in Waswanipi. "You have lots of family there. You'll be welcome, especially since you haven't lost your Cree. And don't forget the pictures you told me about!"

Thomas, Sibi's son, walks toward us. He looks at me with his mother's doe eyes. Thomas leans over and gives me a hug. He exudes a natural grace and serenity. He reminds me of Saint-Exupéry's Little Prince, a tall version with dark hair and a black velvet gaze. He assures me that he is all right. His paternal grandparents offer their condolences. While crying and sniffling into their handkerchiefs. So much sorrow left in Sibi's wake.

A week after the funeral, I have yet to shed tears. I deaden my mind with sleep. If I could, I'd sleep till the end of my time on earth. Free of anger, my consciousness extinguished. After seven days, Sibi comes to me in a dream, surrounded by a golden light. I'm buoyed with happiness, my sister so real, I can breathe in her fragrance. All my love goes out to her, I tell her how unbearable her absence is for me. She listens and smiles. She returns the following night. This time she speaks, tells me she will be gone for a while because an arduous task awaits her.

The next day as with the day before, I walk in joy. My sorrow has vanished now that she visits me in my sleep. Sibi does not return.

After several nights spent waiting, I sink into the void she dug with her grave. Nostalgia for the memory of Sibi is all that floats on the wings of my nights. Ever since, I think of her. Every day. And of my own death. Prepare for it, apply the finishing touches in the profundity of the inescapable.

PART II
THE JOURNEY WITHIN

One may not reach the dawn
save by the path of the night.
                    —Khalil Gibran

15

THE COUSIN
AUGUST 2004

JOHNNY HUMBERT MISTENAPEO runs a gentle hand down my backbone. The contact brings me back to my body, my breathing steadies. I inhale the damp air deep into my lungs.

"A firebird and some caribou…" My voice, tenuous, quavers.

Mistenapeo's resonates, "Wings and hooves, above and below, fire and earth. The Great Spirit and Mother Earth.... Support will be there for you!"

I feel well around this man, serene plenitude flowing into me. An all-encompassing silence.

He adds, "You'll have to let your consciousness expand in the White Cave.... But first you must meet Malcolm Kanatawet in Mistissini."

Koukoum Ka Wapka Oot told us about the Hare's Cave north of Mistissini. Over the last millenia, our Cree ancestors made their tools, arrowheads, and spearheads deep in the heart of the Colline Blanche where the sacred cave is found with its walls of quartz of unequalled resistance and purity. Through Maman and Koukoum, I knew that the ancients used the cave for their ceremonies.

"Noumoushoum," I say, "Who is Malcolm?"

"Malcolm will help you locate George's remains."

Mistenapeo says nothing for a good while to let those terrible words sink into my consciousness. Then he resumes, "His nickname is Caribou Man, Atikh Nabeh. He has developed the ability to track moose and caribou based on the signs that appear on their antlers and horns when thrown into a wood fire. He still thinks and walks like a young man. He'll surprise you. Be careful, he likes pretty women! By the way, are you pretty?"

The old man loves to tease! Speaking of caribou men, I'm reminded of my quest to find caribou-hide moccasins that led me, like a trail, from one community to another, a quest I'd forgotten in all the agitation I've experienced since our arrival in Waskaganish early this morning.

I realize that Mistenapeo is entrusting me to Malcolm to lead me where he cannot follow. Having only known him for a few short hours, I'm taken aback by the wave of sorrow that engulfs me. This man, this stranger, has met me in a place unknown to all my loved ones, a place where I quake with the intensity at the heart of solitude. In the heart of my very essence. Aware of my emotion, the Elder places his hand on my shoulder. He says nothing. Makes no attempt to reassure me. He knows.

"Tell me, Noumoushoum, I have one last question. If my great-uncle's spirit is what needs freeing, why find his remains?"

Gently, he says, "To bring peace to his family members. So they can be freed of grief."

Morning is drawing to a close. By the sun's position, I know it must be noon. I'm starving. I ask Humbert to share a meal at the inn with Stanley, his wife, and us. He accepts. As he leans on his lovely cane, I lead him, my arm beneath his.

Thrilled to be with us, Mistenapeo relegates the man of power to a back seat and becomes the fun-loving prankster who put me at ease this morning. He tells stories of his first encounters with white people. We can all see he's testing Daniel's facility with a comeback. His retorts please the grandfather, whose booming laugh echoes throughout the restaurant. Curious, other customers glance at our table.

I notice one couple staring at me outright. The man gives a timid smile. The woman, her back to me, doesn't dare turn around again. I focus on the contents of my plate. Shirley talks to me about her children, three girls and a boy. The eldest, a girl, is ten. Surprised to learn that a number of our children are in their thirties, and that we're grandparents several times over, Stanley exclaims at our youthful appearance.

Mistenapeo ad libs, "Sex, children! Sex keeps a body young!" Turning to me, "So you're a *koukoum!* That's good. *Koukoums* make the best women of power." His laughter rings out once more.

Our transition to a public setting creates a distance between the two of us. It may be deliberate on his part, but it does feel like he's taking up a lot of space. His jokes draw attention to us. Yet he isn't deaf—the two of us spoke softly down by the river. He's at home here, of course, but I'm embarrassed by the gaze of others. A hunch tells me this man has me figured out. He knows that a huge display of ego displeases me no end. I suppose his actions are designed to loosen the ties of my affection for him.

I excuse myself and leave the group for a minute. I must have brushed against the couple's table because the man aims another timid smile at me. I smile in turn. He waves me over. "Are you Victoria?" he asks in English.

He met me several years ago in the village I'm from. He was living with my brother Demsy and his wife Loussie. His name doesn't ring a bell. So many people took advantage of my brother and his then wife's generous hospitality.

"Allow me to introduce you to your cousin—Victoria!" As though he has just cracked a good joke, he starts to laugh, showing a missing eyetooth. This new cousin with my name radiates warmth toward me. What a funny coincidence. Slim and rather good-looking, she wears her hair short. She used to work for Hydro-Québec but, after a bout of depression, now manages the restaurant at the Waskaganish Inn. "At least I'm home," she says. "I knew Anne in Val-d'Or well, how is she? You look a lot alike, she often mentioned you...."

Anne was Sibi's given name. I sit down next to my cousin, born a Kapassisit, to tell her and her friend the sad truth. They reel with the news, exclaiming, "Oh, no, how can that be? Not Anne! She was so nice, so pretty!"

"That's what killed her," I say, "Too pretty, too naive. Candy for predators."

My rage throws me off-balance. I excuse myself again, my bladder calls.

On my return from the washroom, Brad swoops down on me by the takeout counter. "Hey, Victoria! You're back!" he says in English, then switches to French, "I have something to show you. Come to my studio after lunch, okay? Right now, I'm in a big hurry...."

He pats his shirt and pants' pockets, grabs the waitress's notepad, rips out a page, scribbles down an address with his pen, then holds the piece of paper out to me. "It's at the top of the hill, fourth house on the left!" He grabs a large greasy brown paper bag the woman at the counter hands him and disappears in the direction of the door. No time for me to get a word in edgewise.

Victoria and Norman stop me again. They ask how the other family members are doing. George? Andrew? Edward?

I no longer hear Humbert Mistenapeo's thundering laugh and glance over at the table. Leaning into each other, my friends look like conspirators. Intrigued, I can't wait to join them.

16

DESCENT INTO THE DEPTHS
AUGUST 2004

I GAZE IN AWE at Brad's work of art. The density, lines, and luminosity of his stained glass leave me speechless. Such virtuosity in its design! The scene is one of Canada geese migrating. In the foreground, squatting and surrounded by grasses, are a couple of the web-footed birds so alive it's as though I can feel the wind ruffling their feathers. But no, it was the school janitor opening the side door on one of his rounds.

Standing next to me, Brad waits for my comments. He's somewhat uncomfortable, embarrassed by my obvious interest, unsure how to behave. I smile to put his mind at ease. "It's magnificent, a major work in your career, Brad...."

Unassuming as this tall young man is, he's not expecting my compliment. His talent comes as naturally to him as his *joie de vivre*. Originally a graphic designer, his work suffered for a long time from the influence of the painstaking approach imposed by his professional training. This monumental work of art is proof that his inner artist has been liberated and that he has the ability to use what he has learned to follow his own path. Does he realize that? Happy with my assessment, Brad invites me to visit his studio in the basement of his father's home. We leave the lobby of the neighbourhood school where my friend's art holds a place of honour.

His father is busy braiding thin larch branches, shaping them into geese with wings outstretched. He invites me to sit at his worktable and asks about my trip to James Bay. Like

Mistenapeo, Mr. Wheschee speaks to me in a Cree free of the English terms the new generation tends to resort to while weakening the language. Their habit is one that saddens me as the loss of a millenia-old heritage. I don't often have a chance to speak Cree and am touched by the respect these grandfathers have for their culture.

An impatient Brad almost has to drag me away by the sleeve. "Come see my pieces downstairs! I've started working in a new style—abstract!"

After the traditional cup of tea, I leave the Wheschee family and set out for the museum where Daniel and Stanley will be waiting. The beginnings of a headache tell me my body needs a rest. I need alone time before my second cousin and I begin preparing the next stages of our search for Great-Uncle George's bones. The river lures me with its long, grey sandbank. The air is humid, a sign of rain to come? I walk, I breathe, and the strangeness of this voyage north to my roots overwhelms me with a jumble of emotions I'd thought put to rest. The pain I believed to be under lock and key has been revived. My impatience and aggressive outburst over lunch were simply a sign of my unwillingness in the face of an inevitable journey. Shaman Mistenapeo's power has delivered me to the dreaded depths.

The past, alcohol, neglect, and lost loved ones resurface, the drowned rising from a lake bed. How can I come to a spirit's rescue when I've been incapable of helping the living? When I have no hold over those still with us even now sliding into the abyss? A wave of anguish provokes a howl that's cut off by sobs wracking my body. I sit with my back against a rock, my head and arms resting on my raised knees. The coils around my solar plexus assert their stranglehold, tightening around me like some wild, enraged animal's fangs. Waves of sorrow reach into the marrow of my bones, into my cells, my atoms. A pack of repressed images hurls itself at me. The first time my father hit my mother, staggering, me hearing her cry, "You slept with Jenny! You slept with Jenny!" Both of them drunk. My father's refusal to go after Maikanish who my mother dragged to the hotel with her. It's a late winter's night. I'm afraid my little brother will catch cold. He's only six. I beg my father, but he refuses to budge. Makwashish stumbling home from our neighbour's. Blind drunk! At the age of four. My parents and the neighbours fast asleep, mouths gaping, sprawled on the grass, bottles of homemade wine scattered around them. Sibi, abandoned by our mother the minute we left for school. On our return late one afternoon, we find her clinging to the bars of her crib, milk curdling in her morning bottle, her diaper full of poo and pee. She's sixteen months old. Her crib under a curtainless window on a sweltering September day, her arms reaching for me. The accusations of incest hurled by our mother at my father. To protect her eldest son. How could she not have interpreted the clues, the traces of sperm on our underwear that appeared early each summer only to disappear when Jimmy returned to school? Sibi's rape by Jimmy when she was three, confided to me thirty years later. My blindness, thinking I was the only victim. If I had known, would I have denounced or threatened him to save her? I weep for the loss of my brother who, after his first year in residential school, came home a predator. "I've got a new game," he'd said. But I wasn't to tell our parents on pain of I-can't-remember-what-consequence.... For years now, his fellow students have testified to the horror they lived through between walls managed by the Oblates of Immaculate Mary. Managed my ass! Children scorned, abused, destroyed. My brothers and sisters placed in foster homes where the abuse continued. One starved, the other beaten, manhandled, sexually abused. Our little ones living under the shadow of alcoholism. Our concern as relatives, our helplessness and ignorance. Why? How can we stop the downward spiral, is such a thing even possible?

17

THE TOTEM ANIMALS
AUGUST 2004

A CROW FLYING overhead caws. Curious, it does an about-turn and lands on a log abandoned on the bank of the Rupert River to stare at me. Its arrival brings me back to myself, wrests me from the grip of despair. The bird hops along the sand, prancing, its beak jutting forward and back in a goofy motion. What does it want? Food perhaps? The crow parades in front of me, barely two metres away, like a large tin soldier. It does an abrupt about-face to start all over again, off-balance on one leg. It looks drunk. I'm overcome with laughter, as uncontrollable as the tears that preceded it. I hear an echo of the joyous laughter of the people of my clan out at Pointe-Aux-Vents. My mother's laughter. This laughter from a source I'd forgotten erases my fatigue, my migraine, my sorrow. Koukoum Ka Wapka Oot's words come back to me, "There are good and bad shamans. Some take on animal shapes or enter an animal's spirit."

Cherished grandmother and cherished memory, alive and generous!

Humbert's smile comes to mind in the cascade of my laughter.

"*Tchi a, noumoushoum?* Nile virus? Or bird flu?" I speak to the bird.

It brings its pantomime to an abrupt end, unfurls its wings and, in the velvet whir of take-off, heads for the village.

The crow is right; the hour has come to return to Daniel and Stanley. I have no idea what time it is or how long I've been down by the river. Back at the museum, my husband walks up to me with an angry, or is it worried, look? He thinks Brad is the cause of my red, swollen eyes. Stanley takes pains to show no interest. Daniel and I need to sort a few things out, we've been drifting apart since our arrival this morning in Waskaganish. I invite him to follow me outside so we can be alone for a moment. My explanation turns him around. Yet I still feel a shadow hovering. So I insist until he blurts out what he has to say, "How does it make me look, waiting for you with no idea where you are. Stanley called Brad, who told us you'd left his studio at least an hour before. And that was three-quarters of an hour ago!"

How can I tell him what I was meant to experience on the riverbank? A stranger in a culture whose rules he knows nothing of, Daniel fears ridicule more than anything. Plunged into a milieu whose attitudes are familiar to me and into my maternal language and culture, I hadn't noticed. I didn't pay attention. I let myself be caught up, re-entering my child's skin, free, solitary and grown-up before my time, finding in nature solutions to internal upheaval.... I apologize.

Reconciled and holding hands, we walk back inside to re-assure my cousin. I know that it will be enough for him to see us together to put his mind at ease. Seated at the computer, he has his back turned to us. His long black braid floats along the sky blue of his T-shirt, a colour that highlights his copper tone. I clear my throat to attract his attention. He turns and seeing our linked fingers, flashes a broad smile.

"I've got a surprise for you," he says, pushing back his roller chair. He holds out a sheaf of white paper with the title "Domind's Ancestors" on the first page. He's offering me the genealogy for my grandparents George and Louisa. My obvious glee pleases him. "I thought you'd like a copy...."

Late that afternoon, we say good-bye to Stanley. Where we go next with our project is up to me; he'll wait for my call. We have to drive back south to return our rental van the next day. Since we don't want to be crunched for time, we'll sleep en route. We stop at the craft store to buy my long-sought-for caribou hide moccasins. Mistenapeo is back in his spot with other Elders in front of the store. After lunch, he'd left us with a cursory good-bye, saying he needed a nap, "We'll see each other later."

Beaded in bright colours, the moccasins are a perfect fit, slipping easily onto my feet. Such meticulous work. I thank Shirley for her choice. She sends me a questioning look, *"Tshagun?"* I urge her to speak.

In some confusion, she says, "Is this whole expedition to Stanley's grandfather's old hunting grounds for real? They mentioned it at noon while you were away."

I nod and ask if there's something bothering her.

"No, it just seems so strange. Do you think you'll find anything? My husband's so excited by the project."

"I don't know," I say. "For now, I'm letting events lead me where they will. The only thing I do know is that I want to see this adventure through to the end. I trust Mistenapeo."

Now that I think of it, I still have to bid farewell to the grandfather. Not an easy thing to do. Over lunch, I understood he has diabetes when he refused to eat any refined sugar and his granddaughter Sandra came to remind him it was time for his insulin. This hunch of mine that he'll no longer be here when I next come through, is it real or a reflection of my own fear? All the knowledge that would disappear with him.... Daniel is losing patience, we have to hit the road. On our way out, he walks over to Humbert to announce our departure. The old man shakes his hand warmly and wishes him a safe journey's end. I take a seat in an empty chair next to Noumoushoum. I hold my hand up, fingers apart, signalling that I need five minutes alone with Mistenapeo. He heads for the car. I decide to adopt a humourous tone with the old man. Around us, the other Elders suggest it's time for tea and cookies. They stand and make their way inside Chez Johnny's snack bar.

"Tell me, Noumoushoum, do you like to travel in the form of a crow?"

His guttural laugh rings out. "Ha, ha, ha! Maybe," he says. "When I nod off, I lose all control over my totem animals! They do as they please!"

He seems to be mulling something over. I pick up on his calmness and grow calm in turn. In this shared stillness, his voice goes straight to my heart.

"My daughter, the path to your truth—the one you glimpsed this morning—will not be easy. You've already suffered a great deal; learn to embrace suffering. Free yourself of it and, in doing so, you will become even stronger. In you there is your family, but also two peoples—the red and white. Whatever you think, the white part of you is as devastated as the red. You need to heal both parts of yourself and reunite them. Opposed, they weaken you. United, you'll stand like a rock whatever the storm."

I hold back my tears. His words feel like a battering ram, like the ones used in the past to break down the door to an impregnable castle. They bring to the surface images buried deep in my memory: a bayonet planted in a German soldier's neck, mortar shells and their deafening explosions, the horrendous fear of not making it out alive. God deliver me, these are my father's memories buried deep inside! My five minutes are more than up. I must leave. I take the old shaman's hand in mine. *"Mist'Migwech, noumoushoum … nashtabou'eh tchad'tchiden…."* Thank you, grandfather, I love you very much.

Mistenapeo pats my hand with his free hand. "I know, my daughter, I know…. Go, your husband is waiting!"

18

BEAR STORIES
AUGUST 2004

WHILE DANIEL FILLS THE CAR up with gas at the village station, I head for the snack bar hoping to find some sandwiches. The cook adds lettuce and slices of tomato to the ham between two slices of white bread. I order fries to please my husband, who comes up as I pay. He gets behind the wheel, no doubt aware of my current inability to take us to our destination.

We drive down the gravel road with the sun at our back. It will follow us for a few hours still. I doze off. An abrupt movement on Daniel's part jerks me from the beginnings of slumber. He's braked. I look at him, surprised, questioning. He points at structures among the spruce trees, perhaps tipis. At the entrance made of fine sand, we leave the car and walk down a mossy path. The structures are various representations of First Nations housing: a longhouse, a tipi, a roundhouse, and even a sweatlodge. The shelters' walls are made of moss-insulated jackpine. Plywood nailed across stumps serves as beds. Pop cans spill out of a garbage bin at the entrance. I step into every shelter. Strong energy emanates from each of them, a kind of tangible magnetism. I wouldn't be surprised if the site had been chosen, with Mistenapeo's help, as a cultural training centre for young community members or for tourists.

I feel a weight on my forehead between my eyebrows as though an invisible hand was trying to gain entrance. Not painful, just strange. Immediately, my breathing deepens and intense heat spreads through my chest and hands. There's no longer any doubt, this place is meant for prayer. I go back to the van for my medicine bag and ceremonial objects. Daniel ventures away down a trail leading to a body of water whose lapping waves can be heard. He has never been comfortable with my spiritual practice, nor was my father in the past with my mother's. Is it just a question of different traditions?

I sit down at the foot of the biggest tree, my back to the north, and lay down a moose hide on which I spread out my sacred objects. Then, responding to a call from Spirit itself, one that almost takes my breath away, I empty my mind, offer myself up, and wait for instructions. I take deep breaths, my mind alert. Touch the centre of my being. Immediately, a chant rises through my oesophagus and is taken up by my throat like some bodily instrument that begins to sing. My hands seize the drum and drumstick, and follow the rising notes, initially confused, then increasingly assured and harmonious. No image comes to me, for whom should I pray then? The answer isn't long in coming. The voice takes on Humbert's familiar rumble, "The prayer is for you, my daughter. The Great Spirit has given you your own power song to heal you."

Luminous joy explodes, a balm to the past's open wounds and my familiar sadness. If I have been blessed, may it extend to my family here and now, but also to my ancestors and to future generations. I see a multitude dancing in a shining golden space. Borne away by this unexpected gift of joy, I lose all sense of time. So Grandfather Mistenapeo will not leave me! A conviction nestles deep in my being—whatever the source of the force disguised as Humbert, it will provide support and guide me along this unknown path that beckons. I can still hear my grandfather's cavernous timbre from this morning. Centuries ago. "Support will be there for you...."

I feel heat retreating in waves from my hands and chest. My chant ends. My whole body tingles, prey to a thousand pleasing pricks of sensation. I smile at my well-being. I open my eyes and think I catch a glimpse of a large, dark shape disappearing into the bushes on the edge of the traditional shelter space. I jerk my head up, drawn by the call of a crow perched on the crown of the tree facing me. "Caw, caw," it cries, prancing on the branch. My joyful laughter is its answer. *"Washiya, noumoushoum, mist'migmetch!"*

The sound of footsteps distracts me. Daniel has returned from his walk, a strained smile on his lips. "I saw a bear cross the creek ... it took me by surprise!"

I laugh outright as I return my objects to my medicine bag. Would I end up adopting my Cree people's beliefs or would I chalk these phemonena up to a coincidence or an animal's curiosity just as my father Joseph did when I was a child? Yet since Sibi's death, he's spoken of animals that visit him in his dreams and of luminous strangers who appear at the foot of his bed at night. Despite his age, my father still has a phenom- enal memory and astonishing presence of mind. Even when he looks to be dozing in front of the TV, he'll still answer our questions should one of us drop by the house where he lives, in spite of any misgivings we may have, on his own. He and I have started talking about the constant presence of the bear figure in my dreams and of omens that have come true, like Maman's death, the illness of one of my brothers, another's suicide attempt.

Only Sibi's death was announced differently. I hadn't grasped the message's meaning. Papa is used to long silences. But he likes to share his memories. One time when the two of us were alone, he spoke to me of events surrounding the day I was conceived. At the age of eighty-three, Papa has begun to reveal his inner life to me....

They were on their trapping grounds with my grandmother and her family. It was a cold late November day and a deep layer of snow blanketed the ground. His father-in-law, Sam, was walking ahead when he noticed what looked like a bear's den.

"Sam stuck close to me. I ask 'im to climb up on top of the *washe* to wake the bear, if there's one. I look through the opening up front, see a li'l light movin' inside in the dark, figger it's an animal's eye, so I shoot.... A helluva lot of gruntin' and shufflin' goin' on! I got one cartridge left in my shotgun. I wait for that bear to stick out its muzzle, brace myself good and I got 'im! A whoppin' male! Then I figger out Sam's gone. I look round, no Sam.... I look up and see him almost five hundred feet away, top of a hill. Some quick runnin' he must've done to get there that fast. Some helper!"

They emptied its stomach, tied its back legs together, and dragged it back to camp. My father still gets a chuckle thinking of how scared Sam was.

"I was frozen stiff from head to toe," my father continues. "Our tent was warm with the stove on, but me I'm shiverin' anyways. Then what happens but your mother pushes back the blankets and starts to roll down her long wool stockings. We'd only been married a month by then. She lays on top of me and warms me up somethin' fierce! Ha! M'girl, your mother was never so good as that night! You came into the world nine months later."

Moved, Papa clears his throat and heads over to make some coffee. After he was widowed fifteen years ago, he stayed on his own, ignoring the phone calls and presents from certain lonely women. Despite alcohol's ravages, the love of his life had been our mother and he didn't seek out another companion. He asks if I'd like some coffee. I join him at the kitchen table. He continues his story about the bear.

"Your great-uncle George found two orphaned bear cubs and brought 'em to the Pointe-Aux-Vents camp. The kids gotta kick outta them, you more than anyone, not even a year old. You'd grab onta the cub's fur to stand up and fall on your bum when it moved. Then you'd crawl after it fast as your legs could go. It was like it was scared of you. We all got a good laugh outta that."

Once the cubs grew too big, roasts were made out of them for the late September *moukoushan*, the wind-up to summer when people headed out to the trapping grounds.

19

DANIEL

AUGUST 2004

B ACK ON THE ROAD, Daniel and I agree that I'll drive till darkness falls. He's tired and wants some sleep. The clock shows it's barely six. We'll be in Matagami early enough to have a hot meal tonight in the restaurant at the motel on the way into the city. I like to drive in silence, my gaze on the horizon where clouds cling to the crowns of pointed spruce trees. The landscape inhabits me like music. Softly, I hum the tune of my most recent meditation. Would I forget it otherwise?

We drive south. The sun casts its rays on my sleeping companion, who's oblivious to their continued warmth. He snores. Tenderness washes over me seeing how trusting he is in sleep. His features are childlike despite the small wrinkles at the corners of his eyes and his near-white beard. I'm grateful to him for being here with me. Grateful to life for having met him in our later years after several relationships both tumultuous and calm, and a number of children. He was working for Indigenous economic development programs. At a symposium in Quebec City attended by some three hundred people from different nations, I represented my community's Indigenous centre. A man approached me to congratulate me on the outfit I'd chosen to wear and added, intimidated, "You know, I'd love to be as daring as you. I especially want to tell you how much I love your intense, brazen, and oh-so human poetry!"

He blushed, saddled with the grey wool suit in which he faded to nothing despite the blue of the tie that highlighted his eyes.

I sensed he harboured a secret wound. It felt like I was face to face with a being fragile in both body and soul. Instead of clothing him, his suit disguised him as a civil servant.

The following year, on the first day of another Indigenous Friendship Centre meeting where Daniel sat next to me, he made a date for us to go out for pizza. To talk about literature. He'd pick me up in my hotel lobby. It was September, a hot, sunny day. After a quick shower, I slipped into a light dress. He showed up wearing jeans and a muscle shirt that accentuated the blue of his eyes. On the spur of the moment, I said, "You do have shoulders!" and felt his biceps to check their firmness. It was the first time lightning struck because of a sleeveless T-shirt!

Daniel sleeps on while the heat of my remembering has me melting like brie in the sun. Softly, I sing words by Reggiani, my favorite singer:

"Toi, qui ne seras jamais
Une grande personne
Ne me quitte jamais
Je t'aime..."

Which moves me even more. Daniel wakes just as I'm dabbing at my eyes with a tissue. He stretches and yawns, "Why're you crying?" he asks.

"Because of you, you melt my heart!" I tell him.

"What did I do I exactly?"

"Nothing at all. Don't you ever feel moved by me?"

He smiles. "I get a hard-on whenever you speak Cree."

When I hit him with my balled-up tissue, he's still shaking with laughter and pretending to fend off a much more dangerous attack. What a lech!

I park the car on the side of the road to stretch my legs and take a badly-needed pee. My bladder's suffering from the consequences of early menopause. After a bit of a stretch, we get back in the car. Daniel takes the wheel and turns on the radio. Since he's not a fan of country music, he switches it off again. In a strong nasal twang, I sing,

"Thank God for the radio
When I'm on the road
When I'm far from home
And feeling so blue...."

As a final flourish, I howl like a she-wolf in heat. Now he's the one with tears in his eyes! Tears of laughter.

20

THE LYNX

AUGUST 2004

W E BOOK A ROOM in a motel on the way into Matagami, too tired to pitch our tent or to use our camping gear to make a meal. We want our last night of travel given over to comfort and love's ardour. I've barely stepped out of the shower before I tackle Daniel and nibble the sensitive skin around his neck and shoulders. A gambit guaranteed to drive him crazy.

After making love, hunger pangs set in. Grudgingly, we slip our clothes back on and walk down the hall to the dining room. Daniel offers me wine knowing the effect it has on my libido, and says straight-faced, "Red for my Red?" He knows that white wine knocks me out while red wine revvs me up.

The next morning, I wake from a singular dream. Snuggled against Daniel, I describe it to him.

From the window in the house's north door, I watch five panthers at play. They're sliding otter-like down the snow that's accumulated on the car overnight. I hurry to lock and bolt the door. A woman who looks like me appears and I clearly understand that she is in fact a panther in disguise. I am glad she can't come inside. However, she steps easily through the bolted door. Instantly, the entranceway expands. I'm afraid. Daniel suggests we kill her. I suggest we call the SPCA instead or the game warden. Ignoring me, he comes up with a complicated system whereby the woman will shoot herself. I feel an increasing sense of unease. Meekly, she obeys Daniel. Standing facing me, she stares at me with eyes full of tenderness as she pulls the trigger. The bullet enters through the back of her head and exits out her forehead. But she doesn't fall as blood runs down her face. Just then, I see Daniel behind her, his face all bloody, bearing the exact same wound as the panther woman.

I can feel Daniel's breath on my neck, but he stays silent. An intuition makes its way to my brain. I hesitate for a second before asking him, "Tell me, Daniel, does it bother you that I might become a shaman or may already be one?"

"I don't know," he says, "I haven't thought about it. But you know how I mistrust religion...."

He gets up, heads for the bathroom and turns on the taps in the shower.

On our way to the gas station, we meet Harry, Jos, and Allaisy's eldest son, with his sister Eena and his wife Joyce. Eena, who used to live in our village across from Pointe-Aux-Vents and has kept in touch with my family, introduces me. Harry remembers Tititèche, the Little Little One, and exclaims to see how tall and big-boned I've grown. I vaguely remember him. He inquires after my father's health. "I used to go hunting with him," he says, "He was great!"

He's a slim, good-looking man with bulging muscles and greying temples. I ask how old he is. My question doesn't surprise him in the least. With pride, he raises his whiskerless chin and says, "Seventy-one!" I inquire after Bobby, his younger brother, who liked to tease both Alice and me caught up in our little girl games.

Harry tells me that a good part of their parents' former hunting grounds have been returned to them thanks to the signing of the James Bay Agreement.

"Bobby'd love to see you again, he always thought you were a pretty one even though the two of you were related," he says.

I give Harry a gentle shove and utter a long drawn-out, "Huhhh..." to show my embarrassment. Eena roars with laughter at my typical Cree reaction. Daniel walks over. It's time to leave if we don't want to have to rush.

VIRGINIA PESEMAPEO BORDELEAU

I find it strange this bumping into members of my extended family unexpectedly, as though my memories of them are following me on our trip to James Bay. Seated behind the wheel, I talk about Eena and Harry and recall that part of my childhood for Daniel. We've been driving for a half hour or so when I see an animal's body lying on the side of the road. It looks like a huge cat with a long tail.

"What do you think that was?"

Daniel doesn't know what I mean since, distracted by my story, he didn't see the creature. I wonder if it was a cougar, the large feline some observers claim to have glimpsed in our part of the country over the past few years. "Let's have a look," I say, parking the car. Daniel walks over to the body as I rummage through our portable fridge for some cold water. And fruit, in there somewhere with our backpacks and sleeping bags. The sloppy packing is a sign of the weariness that comes at trip's end. When I finally look up, my husband has vanished. I stride over to what I think is a cougar. It's a lynx! Lying on its belly with its one dislocated hind leg stretched out beneath its pelvis, making it look like a long tail. How is it that this beautiful grown animal could be hit head-on on this straight, flat road?

Daniel's arrival pulls me away from my thoughts. He's coming up a trail that plunges into the jack pines next to the lynx's body. His expression puzzles me. He won't say what he found on the path. Just tells me to go see for myself. Unsettled, my heart starts beating faster. From a distance, I catch a glimpse of three crosses; a familiar mask hangs from one of them. My friend Denis Kistabish, a musican and carver, lies beneath that cross. Under the other two lie his brother Johnny and his father Mathias. I have a connection with the people buried here!

We would visit the Kistabish family whenever our parents took us to the Amos Algonquin reserve. Before he met Maman, Papa, born in La Sarre, used to hunt on Algonquin territory. Although they didn't have much use for him at first, his respect for their people eventually earned him their friendship. He spoke their language and lived the same lifestyle. I even think he dated a few women from their community before enlisting in the army and leaving for the European front. Denis played his drum for me at one of my public poetry readings. We had plans for a multidisciplinary show some day. As for Johnny, a law student, he was everyone's friend. At the time of their death, I was out of the country for seminars and conference presentations. Their niece had told me their ashes were buried on ancestral land, but I didn't know exactly where. Because of a dead lynx and a curious husband, here I stand staring at their graves. My sorrow is equalled only by the joy I feel at finally being able to say my good-byes.

A blue jay snaps me out of my reverie. Reluctantly, I leave the peaceful, soothing spot behind....

I go back for one last look at the lynx, the guardian animal of secrets according to my mother's tradition. Was it my friends' totem? But why had their guardian chosen death to put me in touch with their spirit? Who knows? Lost in thought, I join Daniel who waits for me behind the wheel.

21

THE ACCIDENT
AUGUST 2004

A PLASTIC CONTAINER IN HAND, I crouch down in front of bushes bursting with blueberries, our dessert after sandwiches at lunch. Daniel has parked the car on the side of the logging road. Trucks loaded down with logs raise the fine dust created by the past few sunny days. I half-think how this spot seems far from ideal, but hunger makes my husband impatient so.... He starts walking toward a hill on the road ahead to find a picnic spot. I hear another flatbed truck's engine. I stop gathering berries and shout, "Daniel, let's go somewhere else for lunch, this is no place for a picnic! We'll eat in the car if we have to."

He turns just as two all-terrain vehicles, side by side, barrel down the hill he's on. On their heels comes the truck whose driver does his best to brake, honking all the while. I can no longer see Daniel for all the dust. Yet the truck screeches to a halt just in front of our car. My heart is seized in an icy grip. This can't be happening. God, please no, in God's name, no!

I run, run as fast as my legs weak with terror will carry me. No, he'll get back up again.... Yes, he will, long before I reach the spot where he disappeared.... I scream, "DANIEL, GET UP! GET UUP! I BEG YOU! DANIEL!" I lose my footing on the gravel and slide more than race to his side. He looks to be asleep in the ditch, his head resting on a rock turned red with his blood. What should I do? Not move him, yes, that's it, don't move him.... Check to see if he's breathing, his pulse, yes, on his neck with two fingers.... Blow into his mouth to help him breathe, yes, that's it.... Oh, right, AN AMBULANCE! WE NEED AN AMBULANCE! Once again, I cry out to the blue of the sky stretched above us, indifferent. Blue before. Blue after. Forever blue.

I give a start as a voice thick with emotion answers.

"It's comin', lady, I called 911 on my cell. They're comin' from Amos, nearby ... ten, fifteen minutes max ...."

I'm shaking all over, my teeth chattering and I see ... I see reflected in his face the terror my eyes project. He stares at the ground, arms dangling. He says, "The ATVs passed me on the hill, gotta be kids to pull a crazy stunt like that. When I laid eyes on your husband, he was fallin' into the ditch already. It's not my fault, lady ... not my fault...."

I can see now that he's crying. This young man, the same age as my son, moves me. I thank him for stopping and am touched by the thought of my Simon. Long minutes pass. Through the impatience of waiting, I keep speaking to my husband, hoping he'll hear me, cling to life. My body still trembles and refuses to do my bidding.

The man glances at Daniel and the shudder in his eyes turns my gaze back to my loved one. He has opened his eyes the colour of the sky and focuses them on mine gone misty with mad hope, struck by their blue gracing me with the gentlest light that no firmament will ever bestow. I lean over, kiss his lips. He murmurs, I have trouble hearing him past the shrill wail of rapidly approaching sirens.

"...Didn't tell all ... that love ... life." His voice. Again. Speak to me again! Again! I focus on him with all my might, offering him my breath, my life in exchange for one more word. But the blue no longer flickers. Only seems to shrink then grow dark. I lose myself inside, vaguely hear doors slam and men's and women's voices, a swirling around the two of us. Another siren. Someone puts their hands on my shoulders and walks me away from Daniel.

"Excuse me, ma'am, we have to move him...." I cling to the arm helping me to my feet but fall back to my knees. Then I crawl from the ditch to let the paramedics place the oxygen mask on Daniel's face. They handle him gently, check his vital signs. Endless seconds. Finally, they strap him onto a stretcher, taking infinite care with his head sticky with blood.

"Tell me he's going to live! TELL ME HE'S GOING TO LIVE! SAY IT!" A wild howl born of utter powerlessness. My cry freezes the entire surroundings, even the rescuers' gestures are suspended, slowed by the force of this defiance in the face of the inescapable.

They then transform into emergency specialists again—precise, efficient. After long minutes, they finally slide the stretcher into the ambulance and one of them says to the driver, "Quick, we've gotta hurry! Call the hospital now!"

A squat policewoman walks over. She speaks, but I can't hear her. I'm on the outside of my body, an automaton floating free of gravity. I'm suffocating, gasping for air. A black beast has lodged itself in my chest, is crushing my lungs, its paws casting around for my heart to stop its beating. Death! Daniel! I'm fused to his being that I carry at this exact moment in my lungs. In this second, in the invisible, I witness the departure of my companion, my friend, my lover, my love. I see his fear, his struggle with death, his panic, his call for help. On my knees, held tight by the constable, I inhale, deep into my being and propel with all my strength that same air, open-mouthed, toward the blue of the sky, toward the infinity into which my love's essence soars.

Escorted by Daniel's gentle blue gaze, I re-enter my body and collapse against the policewoman's shoulder. "It's over, over...." Thoughts spoken aloud. Now the woman can guide me to her patrol car, its lights flashing. She buckles a seatbelt around my limp body, speaks to distract me. Do I have any family? Who should she call? Am I able to make the calls? She starts after the ambulance as it races straight ahead.

Within an hour, I'm surrounded by part of my family. Maikan, Édouard, and Margot. Silently, they form a circle around me as though to shelter me from sorrow, from harm. I give myself over to their loyal solicitude, they will look after everything, I won't have to worry about a thing. So I let myself drift, my eyes on Daniel's face, so calm. The emergency nurse on duty has granted me this time for farewells.

I emerge from my comatose state when I realize I'll have to announce their father's death to his children scattered through-out the province. I decide to tell their mother who will know better than I how to respond to their sorrow.... Maikan holds out my husband's address book that a nurse gave him with his other personal belongings. I'm shaking again, so cold, so very cold. Worried, my sister Margot asks whether a doctor should examine me. I tell her it's normal, the shock. Then my daughter's voice, so childlike despite her thirty-some years, weeps into her uncle's cellphone. I have to answer the officer's questions regarding the circumstances surrounding the accident as well. Then the same officer advises me that he's requested an autopsy to see whether Daniel was hit or not.

Amos. Scarcely ten days ago, we bought groceries here for our trip to James Bay. Full of joy, excited at the prospect of striking out on a new road. Today, gone. The void. Nothingness. Noumoushoum's warning, "Your path will be difficult...." Were those not the words he used?

Oh, but Grandfather, not to this extent! The price too steep for the secret revealed by the lynx.

22

THE MESSAGES

AUGUST 2004

I'M DRINKING BORDEAUX. I like its body and dash of meat-iness. Younger, I preferred sharp, peppery wines, but no more. *Red for my Red?* I try to find a new footing. Insomnia. Headaches. When I close my eyes, I see again the mammoth truck bearing down on Daniel. I wish I could cry, but I'm dry, hard and dry. Like black granite. Did I bring on his death by calling out to him?

After three days spent with my family and waiting for the arrival of my children, their spouses, and my granddaughter, I now wait for the autopsy results before going ahead with the funeral. My brother Maikan finally agreed to drive me home, to the house Daniel and I had had such plans for. He wanted to plant fruit trees in one corner; I wanted an art garden inspired by different cultures.

I need to be alone to pull myself together. The animal inside me needs to lick its wounds alone in this setting where happi-ness still hovers over the furniture, the paintings on the walls, the books in the bookcases with their accumulated dust. Not quite drunk, I stand tall as I walk from one room to the next. I touch the clothes Daniel left lying on the floor when we left, breathe in their scent. I caress his tools on the ground by the front door. I speak to him as though he were here and walk into his office. The answering machine flashes on and off. I soak up what was his workspace. His computer. His dictionaries. His research books. I lick the lip of his pipes and breathe in his tobacco. I read the notes he took before leaving for James Bay. His writing, slanted to the left, and the tiny capital letters that always moved me. Would a handwriting expert interpret them as showing an attachment to the past and an unconscious spurning of protocol? Perhaps.

I go back to pour myself another glass of wine. The answering machine in the dining room is flashing, too. I perch on Daniel's favourite armchair in the living room and my gaze is drawn to two prints by a French artist. We were impressed by their exceptional quality at a flea market in Quebec City. The titles and signatures etched in the ink of that period, yellowing and slightly blurred, show their age—1880. The scene is of Millet's house in Barbizon and of Stevenson and Diaz's homes.

The year after we bought the prints, I was invited to Paris for a conference and Daniel came with me. As we walked along the Rive Gauche one day, I saw a poster in a restaurant window. It announced an event in Barbizon. Without even consulting each other, we knew we'd visit Barbizon while we were there. We were staying with our Parisian friends, Évelyne and Pierre. Daniel asked them how we could get to Barbizon. Speaking to his spouse, Pierre suggested, "Honey, why don't we picnic with the children on Sunday in the Fontainebleau forest? We'll take both cars...." Such generous friends!

The next Sunday, we're in Barbizon in Millet's house and studio, now a museum. I drink it all in. And more. A venerable old man with a singsong accent is speaking to Italian tourists about Millet. Slowly, I walk over to the old man and wait my turn to speak to him about Etchard, the man behind our prints.

"He was a friend of Millet's, an engraver," he said. "What was the first name?"

"Just the initial M."

Visibly interested, he tells us he'd need to see our paintings since Marcel Etchard had a son, Maurice, who was also a printmaker, but a less talented one. I ask if the prints would be valuable if they were the father's. He looks at me as though I'd just made a huge gaffe.

We walk out into the sun-drenched street. Our friends bump into neighbours out sightseeing as well and we look for a café to go for a drink together. As we pass a display rack full of postcards, I catch sight of some poorly made copies of our prints. I grab Daniel's arm, "Look! If someone's gone to the trouble of copying them, they must be the father's work, don't you think?"

"Sure looks that way. But what does it matter?"

He'd been right, it didn't matter. Looking down, I notice the answering machine flashing again. "Two weeks' worth of messages, what a nightmare!" I think to myself. I totter over to the machine and hit play.

"Hello, this message is for Daniel. It's Maryse. I've found a book for you. Call me when you get back." Click.

"Hello, Victoria and Daniel. It's Jim here, just wanted to catch up on your news. We're all well. Ciao!" Click.

"Hi, Mom, it's Simon. Happy birthday!" Click.

"Hi, you two! It's Nicole. I dropped Mouski off at Jeannot's, I've gone back to work. Don't worry. The dog's doing just fine. Bye!" Click.

Oh, right, the dog …

"Hello, Victoria? It's Carmelle here. I'm sorry, I can imagine the state you're in, but I need to talk to you. The girls want to know what really happened to Daniel. My condolences." Click.

The present has caught up with me … my step-daughters' mother. Oh, no …

"Hello, Victoria! It's Louise here. I'm so sorry, so very sorry … if there's anything at all that you need, I'm here and Huguette, too. I called everyone in the group. Bye!" Click.

"Hello, Dan and Vicky? It's David Fraser. This message is for Victoria. I've got something to propose to you. Actually, I need your artist's view. Too long to explain here. Basically, we're doing an archeological dig along the Eastmain River before it's flooded and would like to publish some texts on the river and its importance for the Cree. Would you have time to come onsite? You're invited. I'll wait for your call." He gives me his number. "See you!" Click.

David? It's been such a long time since I last heard from the archeologist working for the Cree. The Eastmain River? He's invited me to the Eastmain River? The information takes a while to reach my Bordeaux-saturated brain. I hit play a second time. Once again, David's anglophone accent. I heard right. If Uncle George had been relegated to a back burner because of my grief, tonight he's back knocking at my door. My funny bone is tickled by the situation and I start to laugh. I laugh till I'm rolled into a ball in the foetal position on the living room rug. Then my laughter turns to tears. They take me by surprise, but I don't resist. I open myself at last to my great sorrow, let myself be swept away like a twig in the furious whirlpools of its waters.

23

THE NADOSHTIN PROJECT

SEPTEMBER 2004

O N THIS MIST-SHROUDED September morning, I take to the road again. Keep moving to avoid wallowing in depression. Our lawyer will have to make do without me for the next few weeks; I've given him carte blanche. The trunk of the red Toyota carries what I'll need for a long stay in the forest. I pull on the thick wool sweater my daughter Mylène gave me last year for Christmas. Each gesture reminds me of my couple. How do you live through a first Christmas without "him?" My heart fills with bitterness and, to leave it all behind, I make my mind up to travel outside the country for the Christmas holidays. Right, why not ask my girlfriend Micheline, who's been single for so long, to come with me? It's a perfect time to head for the American southwest—a draw for both of us. She wants to introduce me to a friend who wrote a book on the medicine circle, and some of my father's cousins have wintered there for years....

The dog's barking brings me back to the present. Mouski knows he's going for a car ride and can't wait for me to open the passenger door. My mutt has helped me cope with my sorrow as though he can read my thoughts. He's such a funny creature, who hunts like a wolf and behaves like a sentient being. Every time we pass a semi-trailer, he throws himself at the window and howls in rage. At first, I was taken by surprise, but now I launch a pre-emptive strike: whenever I see a flat-bed truck on the horizon, I sternly order him to stay put. So he whimpers instead. I refrain from drawing any conclusions. He can tell I hate them and that's that!

At Val-d'Or for my scheduled meeting with David, I park in front of his house. I roll a window partway down for air and to make sure Mouski will be fine. Diana, David's wife, opens the door and hugs me in silence. I appreciate her discretion. She can tell at a glance that I've had to answer all kinds of questions about the accident and what my frame of mind has been for the past month. She calls up to David from the bottom of the stairs leading to the bedrooms.

I hear something hit the ground. David comes down yawning, his hair sticking straight up. He smooths it down with one hand, only to have it spring right back again. The gesture makes me smile.

"Hello, Victoria, I fell asleep reading. Sorry to greet you this way ... but I've just got back from up north and I'm tired!"

After giving his condolences, he offers to make me coffee during which time he tells me about the work he's doing on the banks of the Eastmain River. A team of Québécois and American archeologists and anthropologists sponsored by the University of Southern Maine's Department of Geography and Anthropology has been working on a dig of sites the Cree occupied for centuries along the Eastmain River. Elders from the communities affected by the hydroelectric dams guide specialists in their research, showing them where their nomadic ancestors used to stay. Even more importantly, they list the graves of family members who lived on the territory. Should I mention my great-uncle to David? He'll think I'm some kind of crank! He is, after all, a scientist....

I say nothing.

"Did the Elders decide what to do about the skeletal remains?"

David sets a cup down on the coffee table for me and settles into the armchair across from me. His answer is of great interest for my plan's future given that negative results now seem highly probable. Actually, without Daniel here to support me and since my return to an urban environment, George's story has increasingly seemed to be a waking delusion. I've kept on only to honour my promise, or what feels like one, to Stanley and Humbert.

"For them, it's out of the question to disturb the dead. That's the way they put it: *disturb the dead*. We attended ceremonies in each small cemetery in the territory. They planted white crosses decorated with ribbons, flowers, sweetgrass over the graves. A very moving ritual ... even though within two months everything will be under water."

I can imagine the suffering this new bereavement must have awakened for the families. All for the good of the white majority and Americans who will likely offer to purchase the province's electricity surplus. Did the Cree chiefs, signatories to the Paix des Braves Agreement that allowed for the new developments, really believe they were helping their people? Or were they too ready to listen to advisors from various companies, each more ambitious than the next?

Tears well up again. Embarrassed, David asks if I'm all right or whether he should stop.

"No, it's nothing, I was thinking about the families and the graveside ceremonies. Tell me about the project you have for me."

"With the Elders' consent, the Cultural Heritage program team wants to create a site to honour the 'memory' of the Eastmain and Rupert rivers. It would involve a work of art the Cree could gather around in future. We've already approached Brad Westchee, I think you know him, but some would like to publish texts, perhaps poetry, and I suggested you as well as Janet Gull of Chisasibi. If you like, you're invited onsite to participate in the dig with us and absorb the spirit of the site. Is that the right way to put it? You can stay as long as you need to. We'll be working till early November."

I tell David about my encounter with Johnny Humbert Mistenapeo, who's having me go to Mistissini to meet Malcolm

Kanatawet. I also tell him about a "mission" of my own, not far from the Rupert River in fact, without adding any specifics.

"You keep company with men of power..." David says, surprised. "How about that! One day, I witnessed a shaking tent ceremony led by Mr. Kanatawet. I have to admit I was impressed."

I add, "Malcolm Kanatawet is supposed to accompany me to the Colline Blanche. If you can wait, I'll meet up with you after my visit with the shaman. I might bring one or two brothers and even a cousin with me...."

An awkward pause.

David thinks I'm reluctant to compromise my reputation among the Cree who are uncomfortable seeing a lone woman in a group of men. He reassures me that in addition to the male archeologists at the camp, there will be a female cook and students.

"But we're happy for any outside help. Welcome to your family members! Too bad I can't go to the Colline Blanche with you. I suppose you know it's a sacred site for your people? In fact, I have a document on the place and can give you a copy. I was part of developing an archeological research study led by Québec's wildlife and parks society with the Cree Regional Authority to create a conservation park around the hill."

He doesn't insist on finding out why I'll be visiting Mistissini and gives me the name and cell number for the Nadoshtin project coordinator in Nemaska, who will show me around when I arrive.

24

MOUSKI

SEPTEMBER 2004

MY SHETLAND SHEEPDOG cuts a fine figure with a red kerchief around his neck. Driving down country roads, as a matter of course, he sits in the passenger seat and points his muzzle at the windshield. He watches over me. My father used to offer to get us purebred dogs abandoned by officers when they were transferred to other military bases. We kept a Doberman that Maman rightly loathed, a Dalmatian she found bizarre, and a black-tongued Chow-Chow. Papa put a bullet through its head after it had a run-in with a porcupine. Stuck with quills all over, even down its throat, the dog wouldn't let anyone get close. Our favourite, Lucky, a spaniel, lived with us for a long time. One day, he fell under the school bus that he hated and would chase in a rage to keep it from whisking us away. The driver. Mr. St-Arnauld, granted us a few minutes to bid farewell to our friend ... who proceeded to get to his feet and make a dash for the house! Papa took stock of the severity of his injuries and shot him to put an end to his suffering. On Maman's orders, he never brought another dog home.

We're coming up to Makwa's house across from my father's. Mouski pricks up his ears and whines, "Don't worry, you'll get to see Antoine," I say. My nephew and his boyfriend. On hearing Antoine's name, Mouski barks. I've neglected Papa these last few years, busy as I was with married life. Daniel wasn't much of a one for family, or at least not for my family.

We never discussed it, and now it's too late. At the funeral home, Papa clasped me to him, more shattered by my sorrow than his own, then, leaning on his cane, he made his halting way back to his seat.

He's busy by the flowerbeds mowing the grass that still stubbornly grows as fall approaches. He doesn't sow grass seeds, clover takes over from the stubble. Its sweet aroma wafts through the air. Papa doesn't hear the car engine that's drowned out by the lawnmower. Yapping and wagging his tail, Mouski races over and runs circles around him. My father lets go of the mower and turns with a laugh. "Now that's a sight for sore eyes!"

He walks toward me with a slight limp, kisses me on both cheeks and offers up his usual too-strong coffee. "You stayin' for awhile?" he asks.

Right then and there, I decide to stop over for a few days. Try to recoup some sleep after nights drenched with nightmares. Maybe my old bed will work miracles. Papa is happy, "Perfect, I got us some great beans for supper. I'll call the others, maybe they'll c'mon over, too!"

Wonderful idea! My family clan has always done my heart good. Following our father's example, jokes shared around a big table are a surrogate for words of tenderness and affection. A gesture or look tells it all with a certainty embedded beneath our feet in the pre-Cambrian rock.

As I wait for the family, I stretch my legs on the old path that used to lead to Pointe-Aux-Verts, the dog at my heels. He loves chasing squirrels and trapping them on the end of a branch. Then he barks to attract my attention as though he's just hunted down a bear. His favourite game. His instinct helps him detect any real danger. On a hike one day, we came upon two cubs on the trail. I knew the mother couldn't be far off. Thanks to his sense of smell, so did Mouski. He stood at attention in front of me, not making a sound, his lips pulled back, his fangs ready to sink into flesh. He forced me to backtrack in silence. I walked quickly followed by the dog. Once he felt I was out of danger's way, he charged at the intruders, howling like the damned.

On another hike, I spotted the antlers of a lone stag in the distance. I wanted to draw nearer to admire the male from up close. I grabbed Mouski's collar, "Shh! Don't move!" He obeyed. I could feel his impatience shivering across the skin under his fur. Submissive, he kept quiet. He looked up, waiting for the best moment to take off. We were facing into the wind and I ordered him to stay. He crouched by my side and seemed to be admiring the creature as I did. I let him go once the stag noticed our presence and turned its haughty head in our direction. In one leap, it disappeared into the bushes, a silent Mouski racing behind.

My dog came to me through my friend Jean a few years before I met Daniel. Jean's neighbours couldn't stand to see the animal's unhappiness at the end of a leash. I liked Mouski, three years old, from the outset, his short nose under golden-white fur speckled with rust. His expressive eyes, ringed with black as if with kohl, examined me, curious and attentive. Unsure of my abilities as a dog owner, I kept him inside for a few days, using a leash for any outings. I won him over with a lot of patting and dog biscuits. We roamed over the hectares of my land next to my father's at the time; without realizing it, I taught Mouski the extent of his territory. After a week, I unbuckled his leash for our walk. What a champ! Jean came by to see how the two of us were getting on. Recognizing the car, Mouski ran ahead of it, overcome with joy. Before he left, Jean did a bit of an experiment. He opened the back door to his car, his usual signal for Mouski to hop in for a drive. Mouski walked over to Jean, rubbed up against his calves and returned to crouch in the grass at my feet. From then on, the two of us were in it together for life. He replaced my spaniel Lucky; losing him in childhood had made me think I could never grow attached to a dog again.

The memory plunges me back into grief. Will I ever be able to give myself over to love again after Daniel's ephemeral passage through my life? We'd only had such a few short years together.... I'm so tired of death crying victory each and every time as it runs off with those I love. One day soon, my father too will leave us. Then I'll become the eldest, no uncles or aunts left, all gone. They were our "bulwark against infinity" as Mylène put it so well, recounting a dream in which her grandfather died.

Mouski's wet muzzle nestles by my ear. He licks my chin and cheeks damp with tears. "Thank you, my friend." I say, "Let's go back to the others now. Food!" The magic word. He twirls in the air and races ahead of me down the path toward my father's house.

25

MY FATHER
SEPTEMBER 2004

PAPA MAKES EGGS for breakfast; mine are perfect, accompanied with slices of tomato and bacon and beans from yesterday's meal. He has me rehash the circumstances around Daniel's death. A stupid accident. The autopsy revealed only one wound, to the head. The trucker was innocent, as were the careless ATV drivers. Could Daniel's habit of never tying his laces have been the cause of his death? As he backed up, did he trip over a shoelace? Maybe. Half-deaf in one ear, he mustn't have been able to judge the vehicles' exact distance from him. Behind him, the ditch was deep and steep.

During our exchange, my father forces me to speak, to dredge up words lodged in my throat. The affection I glimpse in his eyes, recently operated on for cataracts, moves me. I confess, "Papa, I think the accident was my fault."

Again, I cry.

"Whadda you mean?" His stunned look makes me smile through my tears. I tell him about calling out just before the incident and about my husband's slight hearing problem. He says nothing for a while. He takes time to reflect, standing looking out the window, coffee cup in hand.

"In Belgium's trenches, I was with my buddy Savoie from New Brunswick. He had that Acadian accent, ya' know, in French.... We had loads of fun together. We were sent to spy on a barn we were pretty sure had Germans hidden inside. Bein' scouts, our mission was to spot 'em and force 'em to show themselves. My buddy was a tad absentminded. At one point, I leaned over to dig through my bag lookin' for a biscuit. I heard a shot and Savoie dropped onto me, a hole in the side of his head ... his blood on me. Dead! He'd taken off his helmet, maybe to give his head a scratch seein's how we didn't wash often. Who knows? And he forgot to keep his head down. Seein's how he was blond as could be, they saw him right away."

After a brief silence, he adds, "See, m'girl, for the longest time I asked myself if I hadn't looked for that damn biscuit, would he still be alive today.... Then with time and all the stuff I saw in that war, I figgered out it wasn't my fault. It was just meant to be."

I excuse myself and run for the door to spare him the volcano erupting inside, freeing me of the black mass that has been imprisoned there for weeks. Hidden behind his toolshed, I cry till I can cry no more, with Mouski whining at my feet. A sweet peace radiating heat floods my body and heart.

I go back to my father, who's finishing up the morning dishes. He places a hand on my shoulder, first wiping it on a tea towel, and asks, "Feelin' better now?"

Ignoring our mutual reserve, I hug him, my arms around his neck. "Papa, yes, I feel better. Thank you. Thank you so much!"

He clears his throat. "Ah! That damn Savoie! What a character! I was some mad at those Germans. But now I knew they were in the barn, a small building, more like a cowshed really. I figgered there weren't that many of 'em so I tried my luck. I put my buddy's helmet on the end of his rifle in case they might've thought they missed.... Then slow, real slow, I crawled through the hay the farmers had left standin' 'coz of the war. I detoured way round to the back of the shed. Not much movin' round there. I got close enough to stand up 'gainst the wall and look behind the barn. Get a load of this, one of 'em was standin' there, his back to me, pissing behind a door five, six feet away, real close! I laid my rifle on the ground and pulled out my knife; two strides in and the German soldier was done for, his throat slit! I didn't take no chances, threw my two grenades inside before I made my way in. There was just one other fella layin' next to a l'il window facin' me and Savoie's position. He wasn't a pretty sight! I dunno which of 'em took out my buddy, I'll never know. But at least that day my infantry unit could advance a few more miles into occupied territory. Go figger, they always sent me out scoutin' alone to spot Germans after that...."

I ask if he'd been a scout from the first. He gets a faraway look in his eye, he's back in his soldier's life. "Uh-huh, I volunteered for it straight off. The guys said I walked like an Indian up to no good. Not a sound!" He laughs remembering.

My father's horror stories are part and parcel of our life. He couldn't forget. So he talked. Maman told me when he got back from Europe in 1946, he drank so much he'd have waking dreams. She said he was bewitched. He suffered from delirium tremens. A young nurse managed to free him of his visions by plying him with chicken broth. When he left the army, he bought hunting rifles, traps, a tent, and a canoe, and travelled by train to La Reine in Abitibi. He returned to his poaching trails on the Ontario side and, for the most part, in Algonquin territory. He lived like a hermit for a few years, seeking peace in the vast forests of northwestern Quebec. Tracked by an RCMP officer who just wouldn't give up, he boarded another train to Senneterre. There he met Samuel Wescutie, the Algonquin married to the woman who would become my grandmother Louisa. Sam was getting old and looking for a hunting and trapping partner on his territory. Maman and her son Jimmy lived with her grandmother in Waswanipi.

Whenever Papa tried to describe to us how grim his life had been, he'd exclaim, "I came into the world on a Friday the thirteenth by the Calamity River, then my mother went and died two weeks later." Despite his jesting tone, he was scarred by the truth. Born in La Sarre during the Spanish influenza, he was raised in Champlain by his maternal grandmother and his aunt Madeleine. For the longest time, he kept it a secret that his father went mad after his wife's passing and lived in an asylum until his death. I was eight when I learned that I had a grandfather.

The next morning as I lay in a deep sleep, my sister Élizabeth's voice merged with my dream. She's the queen of our father's heart, his lastborn. True to his desire to give his children names from England's royal family, Papa did, however, concede in the face of my adolescent protests at the arrival of Margaret, Édouard, and Élizabeth, to make André and Édouard's names more French. Albert-Maikan inherited Queen Victoria's spouse's name, a man Papa held in the greatest esteem. André-Makwa was born the same year as Prince Andrew and so bore his name. Margaret was changed to Margot in memory of a blonde German girl who fell for Papa in Berlin. Papa's hopeless anglophilia dates back to his marriage to Maman. People in the village didn't take well to the union of a white man and a "savage" and we were often the targets of racism. Among other instances, Papa was refused a grant offered back then to those interested in acquiring land for farming. The land agent reproached him for not attending mass on Sundays. Papa developed a virulent antipathy toward the Catholic Church and Maurice Duplessis' politics. We were the living proof of his resistance.

From the kitchen, Élizabeth exclaims, "What? Still in bed? It's noon!" Then the hum of my father's voice, likely telling her about my grief and fatigue. My sister lowers her pitch. Hearing the time, I get up grumbling and pull my wool sweater over top of my pyjamas. As soon as I step out of the bedroom, Lizbeth falls into my arms, "Here she is, my sister, I'm so happy to see you! How are you? I brought us lunch. But maybe it's breakfast you're wantin'? You sure look pooped!"

She bursts into laughter. A laugh that brightens up this rainy day. She couldn't be here for bacon and beans the other night, and now she takes up all the space with her youth and vitality. I give a snort and slip into the shower while Papa makes some fresh coffee. I hear him say, "Wait and see, I'll make her a cuppa that'll wake her up good!" Again my sister's laugh. I smile as I turn to the warm water's caress.

Two dreams return, here I go dreaming again! The first, rather muddled, is about Daniel minus the painful fact of the flat-bed truck. The second brings me back to my coming journey. In it, I'm on the road to James Bay again with Uncle George's ashes. When I empty the urn's contents into Rupert River's waters, my uncle materializes saying, "Don't forget your mission!"

Lizbeth serves us her famous Italian pasta dish. She makes everything from scratch, never buys ready-to-serve food, winning the esteem of our food-loving father, who reheats in the microwave the dishes she brings him. My calm restored, I tell them about the Cree shaman Mistenapeo and my upcoming meeting with Kanatewet in Mistissini.

"Both *mitawiou*," says my father. "So you've got the gift and aren't just a dreamer?"

I wonder if he's making fun of me. But, gazing out at the trees dripping rain behind the kitchen window, he seems to hesitate then, remembering an anecdote, discloses an essential part of his origins that we his children knew nothing of.

In response to Élizabeth, who asks why he's kept it secret, he says, "I didn't figger it was important for you lot!"

"But Papa," I say, " that means you're Métis and your mother, too! What nation was your grandmother from?"

Born in Michigan and adopted into a family from Champlain, he thinks she might have been Ojibwe or Mohawk. My sister, whose skin is brown and hair and eyes black, interrupts, "It also means we're more red than white! Now I see why you're attracted to Indian women!"

She laughs, her lips open wide over white teeth. For the past few weeks, Papa has been seeing an English-speaking Algonquin woman who's eighty-five and lives in the seniors' home. "You been hidin' anything else?" she asks.

Papa chuckles. His grandmother Marie-Louise used plants to heal the sick. "When the doctor didn't work out, people'd come to see my grandmother. They say she was a real good healer, the funniest part is she was quite the Catholic. In turn, my grandfather Élie Gouin healed horses. He was s'posed to hand his gift down to me, but I was still too young when he died. Ah ... but he sure spent a lot of time rockin' me!"

"Is he the one who sang all the old songs from France you used to sing to me? *Les sabots de Marjolaine, Le joli mois de mai, L'âne à Marianne?*" He smiles.

I remind him of the time I was a child shaking with a bad fever, lying under a big duckdown quilt. He was sitting by my side. All of a sudden, I found myself on the ceiling, watching him two metres below me. Afraid and trembling, Maman stood in the doorway. Papa put his head in his hands and started to cry. I re-entered my body. Bone-tired. But with the fever broken, I opened my eyes to see my father.

"Your love and sorrow healed me, Papa, they might even have resuscitated me! And you say you don't have a healer's gift? You're the one who transferred your gift to me!"

Papa doesn't know where to look. Mouski barks. Now that the rain has stopped, we hurry outside to see what he's barking at. Édouard's and Margot's cars are advancing down the long drive to the house. I forgot today is a holiday.

26

POINTE-AUX-VENTS
SEPTEMBER 2004

O N THIS SUNDAY MORNING, I push my father's canoe into the water. Sitting in the middle, as good as can be, Mouski scratches his ear. Forty years have passed since the last time the extended family camped at Pointe-Aux-Vents. I tell Papa I'm off for a pilgrimage as I stuff a sandwich and apple into my backpack. And make sure not to forget the dog biscuits. The points of land that advance into the river belong to a logging company now. I paddle slowly, breathing in the tranquil sunny morning. Mouski shatters the silence barking at crows riding the gentle breeze. My thoughts unfurl like waves. Single again, worse yet widowed. What a horrible word. What will I do with our house? Of course, we had a circle of friends, but they were mostly Daniel's. A nomad by nature, I can't see myself putting down roots in a village far from my family who, I've realized today, I miss a great deal.

We arrive at the second point where the Wescuties tented. Their mother, a second cousin of Maman's, married her father-in-law Samuel's brother, a gentle, quiet Algonquin man. Later that autumn, they made their way up the Nottaway River toward Shabogama Lake as far as the mouth of the Magiscane River where they set up camp for the winter. Sturgeons come to spawn there in the spring. My parents would dip their wide-mesh nets into the river to capture the monstrous fish.

We're drawing close to the spot where our log cabin stood. The area is overrun by trees. Big rocks crop up from under the water's surface and I wonder whether my parents had trouble landing. A memory returns: Papa built a dock next to a spring we used for our fresh water. I discover a grassy cove where I wedge the canoe. My boots sink into the mud, and I grab at alder branches to free myself. Mouski disappears up a rocky slope, sand cascading under his paws.

The raspberry bushes prick my hands. I hadn't remembered it being this steep. I'm surprised by how narrow our point is. I remembered an expanse it never had.... I trip on the metal vestiges of a mattress. On the shrivelled end of a jack pine's branches, a rusty, hole-ridden pail hangs. I poke my toe into the ground between the grasses and the raspberry brambles to locate the foundation's remains. Nothing. The earth seems to have swallowed our entire home. The dried-out treetop on the huge birch that Jimmy and I used to climb is evidence of its life drawing to a close. I head for the path down by the rocks where Maman used to rinse her laundry, and by the boulder that Philou knocked himself out on after slipping on a bar of soap. Maman plunged his head underwater to bring him to! My eyes turn to the opposite bank where the Lamarches' sawmill used to stand, now long gone. In front of me lies the water on which my father looked to be dancing on floating logs under my mother's loving gaze.... My emotions gallop unchecked like horses delivered from their stalls. It's time to head to Pointe-Aux-Vents.

Since Mouski vanished the minute we arrived, I climb into the canoe alone, assuming he'll find me by following my scent. As I paddle past Maman's rock, Mouski races down the slope. He barks, desperate, thinking he's been abandoned. I use my voice to reassure him. He runs beside the bank wading through water, not taking his eyes off me. His role as my protector is not looking good. I land on a tiny sandy beach by the bedraggled birch trees whose leafy branches used to keep us hidden from those we spied on across the way. The same place where Angélique breathed her last and Daisy gathered mussels. Tree roots hem in the stones that lay scattered across the beach back then. The climb is tough. I have to push away birch and aspen branches that crowd the space where our Cree cousins' and Algonquin friends' tents used to stand. Retracing my steps, I walk along the shore on the west side of the point toward the fine sand slope we used to slide down on our buttocks. I'd return home, the seat of my pants all golden, my stomach weak from so much laughter and shrieks of joy. My memories bring a smile to my lips.

The silver flash of a pike cleaves the river water. I eat my lunch leaning back against a tree stump. Words jockey for position while I concentrate and wait, my red notebook on my thigh. Lying in the sun, Mouski flicks his ears to shoo away the flies buzzing around him. The poem flows like water in a river set free from winter's grip. My next collection will be a reflection on Pointe-Aux-Vents and lost love.

On my return early that afternoon, Makwa has installed his tools on the porch next to my father's old outboard motor. Catching sight of my nephew Antoine, Mouski twirls in mid-air with joy. Of all our dogs, he's the only one to have mastered this trick. My brother laughs out loud. "Have I gotta good story for you about that dog of yours," he says. "Comin' home from work last night, I stopped off at the tavern. Ti-Jos Cossette was there. I told him about Mouski, how he's real smart and funny, all that stuff. Liar that he is, I couldn't help wonderin' what he'd come out with to one-up me. Wouldn't ya' know...."

Makwa laughs for a few seconds. "He says he used to have a dog that hunted for him. Ran off every morning to bring 'im back a hare, a partridge, a muskrat, all that stuff. One morning, he came back with a beaver. A beaver so big he hadda stick fence posts in it and roll over it with his tractor to get at its fat!"

My brother André-Makwa belongs to a liars club that gets together at chance encounters in the Hunter's Tavern. Losers treat the winner to a beer. Jos Cossette is the club's uncontested champion, what sets him apart being the fact he believes his stories and doesn't think twice about pounding on the table to make his point. "Holy hell, you callin' me a liar?"

Our laughter stops when Maikan's jeep pulls up, greeted by the dog's barking. He has his wife Léa and their grandson Darryl with him. Albert-Maikan and Édouard chose Cree partners, while my other three brothers fell for the charms of my blonde blue-eyed sisters-in-law. The day before, Édouard had already agreed to accompany me to Nemaska, now it's Albert's turn to confirm his participation.

27

EN ROUTE FOR MISTISSINI
SEPTEMBER 2004

AFTER A FEW DAYS' REST, I leave early this morning without Mouski. My father has offered to look after him until my return. Maikan has brought copies of the pictures I'd promised to our second cousin Anna at Sibi's funeral. I wanted to surprise her when we reached Waswanipi, but yesterday my brother told me she was expecting me for lunch. The surprise will have to wait for another time.

I already miss my dog. His presence, so alive and attentive. In some way, he's taken over from Daniel, providing emotional security. Before Daniel, I lived in a chalet on the edge of the forest and only Mouski shared my life. In the summer, a porcupine would come to gnaw on the porch every morning as I ate my breakfast outside, basking in the rising sun. A skunk lived underneath, indifferent to our presence. After one painful, smelly experience, Mouski left it alone. The skunk liked to remind him walking by, its tail held conspicuously high. There could have been no better guard against potential burglars. A red fox liked to chow down on mice or deer mice a few metres from where we sat, not too close after all, to ensure it could beat a quick retreat to the forest if need be. I suspected that my dog had a bond of friendship with the fox and worried about the potential of his contracting rabies. So we showed up regularly at the vet's for every vaccination appointment. One day, I found the fox lying by the road, hit by one of the neighbours who drive at breakneck speed. I gathered up its body and buried it in its native forest across from my chalet.

Lost in thought, I cross the bridge to Rapides-des-Cendres, my birthplace. I park along the river where an old sawmill used to be. Back then, the Algonquin camped on these shores. They gave me the name Ashigon Ikwesis, Bridge Girl. The midwife who helped Maman was Algonquin, as was my godmother. They have always maintained an unshakeable bond with me. Over the years, I've received talismans from one, beaded moose-hide clothing from the other. Those treasures burned with all our other keepsakes during one memorable bender when Maman, drunk and half-asleep, started a fire with a lit cigarette. Fortunately, she was alone. She spent four months in intensive care, her body naked and raw. Not even that was enough to convince her to stop drinking though. Papa harboured that hope during the year of her convalescence. His love grew and he took gentle care of Maman. She'd even been expecting at the time, but she had a miscarriage. Maman had two main traits: resistance to pain and loyalty to her demons, despite Papa's and our love.

The sudden rush of blood as I remember my mother leaves me shaken. I find myself in an altered state, the river's turbulent waters call out to me. I jump to my feet, run up the hill, and throw myself into the car. I choose a country music CD to lighten my mood and sing along at the top of my lungs to chase away the memory of grief. I'm alive! Death can wait, whatever the pain of fourth-degree burns. Next stop, Waswanipi!

My cousin greets me on her doorstep. She's radiant, her beauty accentuated by a red blouse enlivened with a pattern of white flowers. She motions for me to enter first. I'm surprised to find a dozen people seated around her large dining room table. I recognize her sisters Sarah and Sally. They introduce me to their spouses, children, and grandchildren. Anna has been living alone since her husband's death. They look at me, intimidated. My second cousin says, "We heard about your husband...."

They lower their eyes. "*Tante mag etout'teinn?*" Anna asks about the purpose of my journey to lessen their unease.

"*Nistoum n'wimitsoun'!*" I tell her. I want to eat first!

My touch of humour having broken the ice, everyone takes a bowl from the kitchen counter and dips a ladle into a pot of thick soup. I gorge on bannock as fragrant as my mother's. Between mouthfuls, I answer their questions about my family, my children. Suddenly, I remember the album left out in the car and excuse myself. The women have already begun to clear the table by the time I get back so I ask Anna to return to her seat then place the picture of her sitting behind Jimmy in a canoe—she's smiling at the camera. She must be about ten. The others crowd around to look at the images with her. Warm laughter rings out, then silence. Anne spreads the pictures out, making the occasional almost inaudible comment. "*Noutah*," she says, touched by the image of a group made up of my grandmother, my mother, her cousins, her mother, and her father, George.

Her brothers-in-law have to go back to work, one to the band council, another to a new-home building site. They shake my hand. "It was a pleasure to meet you!" Behind them, the teens and youngs adults jostle, eager for a lift.

By three, I'm on the road to Mistissini. My thoughts turn to my second cousins. The three sisters, who'd been filled in by their nephew Stanley, peered at me, curious about the strange mission I was about to embark on, however unwillingly. Sally summarized our words and my doubts. "If you find our father's remains, it will do me good to know where he is … and to complete his skeleton in the cemetery next to Maman's."

Last night I was on the phone with my childhood friend Clarisse who works for Cree Health Services in Mistissini. She's part of a team that develops programs for clients struggling with illnesses linked to diets too rich in fat and sugar. As a teen, I often sought refuge at Clarisse's home where I'd spend weekends talking, laughing, crying. We slept together on the old mattress in her tiny room. We braided each other's hair that danced down our backs, hers light brown, mine almost black. Her parents let us cross Tiblemont Lake by canoe. We brought a snack with us that we tore into after our swim. Her father, like mine, believed that children learn better on their own. During my separation from my first partner, she welcomed me into her big country home where she lived alone with her first son. We led a calm existence there with our children and friends, who'd drop by in the evening and share in our Scrabble games, our gourmet meals. I moved out when she met a new lover whose child she was expecting. Clarisse's love affairs, like my own, don't last.

In Chibougamau, I buy groceries to have something to contribute to the meal. I also buy some local cider and wine. I don't know whether or not alcohol is banned on the reserve as in Chisasibi or Waskaganish. The bottles disappear into my backpack.

28

CLARISSE

SEPTEMBER 2004

CLARISSE LIVES in a big two-storey house provided by the community to non-Indigenous employees. She's waiting for me, the table set for a banquet. We cry in each other's arms. Clarisse was overseas in northern Europe when Daniel died. Two years earlier, weeping at Sibi's funeral, she said to me, "What can I do to comfort you over all this, dear Victoria?" She laughs through her tears, happy to have me here. She's grieving for her mother who died early this year. Both of us are bruised and shaken by life.

I unpack the groceries I chose for their luxury factor—smoked salmon and imported *foie gras*. The menu she has planned includes caribou offered by her boss. At least, our taste for good food hasn't changed. Despite the high suicide and alcoholism rates in Mistissini, Clarisse tells me it's impossible to stop young people from buying liquor in Chibougamau. So its ban on the reserve has had little effect.

I tell her why I'm passing through and she gives me information on Mr. Kanatawet. "He's one of the Elders who help us with the health program. Researchers from Laval University have benefited from his wife's knowledge of medicinal plants. It will be a pleasure to introduce you to him. He's probably expecting you ... the other shaman has no doubt contacted him. But tell me about you. What do you have planned for the future, if I can put it that way?"

I don't know what to tell her. Gazing off into the distance, I wonder again whether I should sell my house. Clarisse's gentle voice brings me back.

"Last week, my boss Glenna told me I could work out of the Montreal offices or from home if I wanted. A new job. I could work via computer, wouldn't have to meet with clients anymore but would travel around the country sometimes for training." Her eldest son, who rents her house with his girlfriend, wants to go back to school. Clarisse doesn't like either city life or the loneliness of country life. "If you'd like, you could move back in with me. Not that you have to ... but I confess," she says with a laugh, "that I really missed you when things with Paul went south! You could write in the garage that's been converted into a workshop. No phone. It's full of light and has a view of the lake. My son put in a wood stove to make it nice and cosy! My godson, an electrician, installed plugs, ceiling lights, and baseboard heating under the windows. If you moved in, I'd always have someone at home to look after the dogs and cat, that is, if you don't end up travelling at the same time as me."

I'm tempted by her offer. For one, it would bring me closer to my family.

Clarisse has had four love interests, the most recent dating back five years. Taken for a ride by her last lover, she now masquerades as a harpy around any suitors. As for me, Daniel came on the scene after six previous lightning-bolt love affairs. "If you fall in love again," I tell her, "will you kick me out just like last time?"

She laughs, her golden eyes sparkling. She maintains that she no longer wants to share her space with a stranger: from now on it will be each to his or her own home and nothing but romance-filled dates. "In fact," she adds, "who says it won't happen to you again given your crazy heart?"

I smile and serve her seconds of roasted vegetables *au gratin* as she fills my glass with red wine. "If I have to wait fifty years to meet another Daniel, I'll be a hundred years old, my girl!

We'll both be fairly wizened by then, maybe even scattered to the four winds long before that!"

We choke with laughter.

Snuggled in my sleeping bag, still a bit drunk on laughter and wine, I think of Clarisse sleeping in her room across from mine. Despite the hurts that plague me, I thank life for granting me a constant, unconditional presence such as my friend's. Not that she's the only one, of course, but no one else knows me as well as Clarisse, who cried with me back when I was bloodied and twelve.

29

MALCOLM AND PATRICIA
SEPTEMBER 2004

I ACCOMPANY CLARISSE for her morning exercise, a quick walk around the mercifully small village. Short of breath, I continue yesterday's conversation. "Clarisse, do you think that grief helps us grow? Do you think we can heal from an abused childhood? Do you think we'll ever grow up, really grow up one day? Or will we spend a whole lifetime getting there?" With a sidelong glance, I see her smiling at my seven a.m. questions. She has small, pretty teeth with a bit of a gap between the middle incisors and a dimple in each cheek that make her look like an eternal child.

"Don't know, my girl! We pretend to in any case! We're all just a bunch of children who've been hurt in one way or another and pretend to be adults. How about we save the topic till tonight? We'll stop in at Jessie's for breakfast, she works with me. You'll love her! She knows the Kanatawets well, and if you want some inside scoop before meeting them, the time is now."

Love Jessie? That's a given! Shorter than the two of us by a good head, she radiates such benevolent energy that I feel like snuggling into her arms so she can rock me. What's come over me? When Clarisse introduces us, Jessie says she's heard of me and is proud of the work I do that reflects positively on the Cree people. Jessie reminds me of Koukoum Louisa, making it easier for me to understand my earlier impulse. She says "Clara" instead of "Clarisse." A colossal man with straight, dishevelled hair stands making toast. This is Richard, her husband. He shakes my hand and welcomes me in English.

"Eggs? Pancakes? Toast? Tea? Coffee?" He lists off his breakfast offerings. His wife laughs and takes over in the kitchen. She tells us he's only good for making toast. Clarisse removes two placemats from a drawer under the table like someone who knows her way around. Richard offers me coffee in a white china cup that looks tiny in his large hand.

According to Jessie, shamans like Malcolm Kanatawet, although respected in the community, generally earn reproving looks from the Anglican and Pentecostal pastors and the Catholic priests. The war to win pagan souls is still being waged on reserves, even though the clergy no longer have the influence they used to have over the first generation of converts. In removing children from their families by force for the purpose of instructing and deculturating them, what the Church and State taught Indigenous peoples was to reflect on the abuses of colonialism. So Malcolm Kanatawet spent twelve years in a Sault Ste. Marie residential school in Ontario. During a group movie outing at the age of eighteen, he caught sight of a young Ojibwe woman. His heart thrilled. Once the film was over, he quickly threaded his way to the exit to speak to her. His stay in the federal residential school ended in June of that year and they were married a few months later. Together ever since, they took up the shamanic practice after training as a medicine man and woman. They regularly take part in First Nations' spiritual gatherings and now teach in turn. In Mistissini, their role involves re-establishing the tradition of respect for Elders, nature, and life in general. "They're very ... very powerful," Jessie concludes.

We make our way to the Kanatawets'. It's almost nine and my friend doesn't want to be late for work. Before she rings the bell, Clarisse deems it advisable to give me a warning, "Mr. Kanatawet is quite the looker! Surprisingly so, you'll see. Women flock to his workshops, but not the guys, go figure!"

She laughs at her own joke as she rings the bell.

The woman who greets us isn't Cree. Tall with greying hair in braids, sharply chiselled features, high cheekbones, a proud hooked nose over thin lips, her appearance is in stark contrast to the usually rounder faces of my people. Her green gaze impresses me—warm, dark, and keen, it seems to see beyond my outer shell. She imprisons my hands in hers, warm and dry. Their warmth penetrates my skin like a faint electrical current, an instant breath of tranquility. I'm face to face with a true woman of power. A Métis woman. Clarisse brings me back to the present with a quick peck on my cheek, then hurries off. We'll see each other again outside her office for lunch. I watch as she walks off down the street.

Her voice a deep alto, Patricia Kanatawet speaks in English. "You're Blue Bear Woman," she says. "I'm honoured to meet you."

I gasp. She has just referred to my totem and its colour, the blue bear that haunts my dreams and has guided me for so long. The totem that struck fear in my mother, who refused to acknowledge it despite the burning desire I had to speak of it. "No," she said," it's not possible! You're just a little girl! The totem's too strong for a mixed blood. No, stop telling me your dreams! You have to live in the white world!" I can still hear her words in Cree that denied my nature and forced me to keep quiet.

"Your mother was frightened by your power and tried to protect you from it."

I can hear sounds coming from the basement, then an extremely handsome man, slim and Cree, appears in the stairway leading upstairs. Dressed in an orange-and-brown plaid shirt, his jeans hug round, firm thighs. He emanates virility and a power that strikes me in the lower belly. Yet he's no longer young, despite his barely silvered hair tied at the nape of his neck. His full lips open in a smile, his exquisite dark hands reach for my shoulders. He, too, speaks in English. "How do you do, Victoria? Humbert talked to me about you. Welcome to the Universe!"

Patricia gives a deep-throated laugh. These two are definitely at home in their bodies, running counter to my biases as a Christian who converted to shamanism late in life. Both firmly grounded and vibrant!

30

THE CEREMONY
SEPTEMBER 2004

THE KANATAWET COUPLE and I sit in a large room in the basement of their home. Ceremonial objects are everywhere, lying on the ground or hanging from the wall—drums, rattles, medicine pouches, herbs in plastic bags. The scent of tobacco and sage wafts through the air. The healing ceremony began several minutes ago. Behind me, Patricia softly beats a drum. Facing me and holding an eagle feather, Malcolm cleanses my aura with the smoke rising from bitter-smelling herbs burning in a shell. The sound of a rattle joins the drum. Somewhat anxious, the sound reminds me of a rattlesnake. Yet I agreed to their suggested "cleansing," the word the shaman uses. He said, "For the ceremony in the White Cave, you have to be free of negative emotions, otherwise your visions will be affected."

My sense of unease grows as though I'm about to lose something essential, life itself. My thoughts scrabble around inside my brain. I sense that I'm close to reaching an unbearable level of anguish. I want to run away. In a husky voice, unlike the one he used only half an hour ago, Malcolm rivets me to my chair. "A spirit stands next to you, a man who has just died, who is he?"

My entire being startles and tears run down my cheeks that I'm incapable of making any attempt to wipe away. I don't know whether my words are spoken out loud or not, "My husband ... an accident a few weeks ago."

The instruments accelerate the beat to an alarming pace. Malcolm lays a hand on my knee, his touch bringing instant calm. His voice is a blend of kindness and authority. "Let him escape into the Universe. Don't hold him back. His place is no longer here with you."

My feeling of loss deepens. Kanatawet lays one hand on the front of my chest, the other on my back. A shard of ice pierces me, anguish replaced by a sharp pain immediately followed by wild, reckless sobbing. Part of me watches from a distance as my being empties itself of sorrow, casting off, shattering all resistance and defences.

How long have I sat here shedding what seem like unending tears? I weep for Koukoum Louisa, Clarence, Jimmy, Maman, Sibi, Daniel. As pain sets fire to my solar plexus, Malcolm lays his hand there saying, "It's all right, it's over." This time, his hand radiates heat that spreads from my belly to the rest of my body. My sobbing ceases. I'm spent. My eyes refuse to open, the salt from my tears burns my eyelids. The drum and rattle sound no more. Patricia helps me to my feet and guides me to an adjoining bedroom. She hands me a glass of water, then tucks me in as though I were a child, telling me to sleep for a while. I have never before felt so liberated. A hollow forms beneath my diaphragm like the one I felt forming inside every time I gave birth.

I float, half-asleep. In my dream, I skip through a field of co-lourful flowers. I can hear myself laughing like a young carefree girl. A telephone rings, wakes me fully. Someone knocks on the door to the bedroom. Patricia's handsome, smiling face. "It's Clara. She'll eat here with us, okay? I invited her. Malcolm wants to tell you something before lunch."

Still slightly woozy, I join the shaman in the ceremonial room. He looks at me with tender irony, my face must look pretty bad. He tells me he has just done a huge amount of work with me, something that usually takes much longer. My excellent health and openness to the mission my great-uncle's spirit has entrusted me with convinced him to proceed, as well as the strength of my totem. "We'll go to the White Cave tonight—spirits like the dark and a full moon."

Clarisse and I leave the Kanatawets. I have the key to her house where Malcolm suggested I rest up. We'll leave later this afternoon. I'm to bring warm clothes and my sleeping bag. As we're about to leave, Patricia stops me. Her green, piercing gaze envelops me with compassion.

"*N'moui esh'k katapegoushan ... Nit'i wabamaw ka wabasitt Maikan nabeh. Egoudeh outem'. Petiyï....*" She tells me to be patient, that I won't be alone, a white wolf man is on his way to me. A man who will respect my ancestors' ways.

I ask her if he'll be from my people. "*Kiti Eenou, ow?*" She refuses to say anything more. I don't insist and hug her to me. Malcolm comes up, not making a sound. He tells me again to make sure to rest. Too bad he's in love with Patricia since I'd like him to be my White Wolf!

Both of them burst into contagious laughter. They really can read my mind!

Blushing, I rush outside followed by a surprised Clarisse, who can't figure out why I'm embarrassed or what they're laughing at. The fresh air does me good.

31

THE WHITE CAVE
SEPTEMBER 2004

WE LAND ON THE BANKS of the Témiscamie River link-
ing the lake of the same name to Albanel Lake. The
late September twilight announces a cold night. I'm wearing
felt-lined boots. On the bank, Malcolm lays out our three-
star sleeping bags, our lightweight self-inflating mattresses, a
backpack full of sandwiches, fruit, and a thermos of hot tea.
Patricia and I grab the rolled mattresses and sleeping bags while
Malcolm shoulders the backpack. He grabs his huge medicine
bag with one hand and mine with the other, then heads toward
the Colline Blanche whose summit with its patches of white
emerges behind a row of spruce trees. Patricia follows close on
his heels. The moon shines round above the coniferous forest.
I recognize the feeling of plenitude inside, the same one I had
with Humbert Mistenapeo. My breathing finds its source deep
below my navel. Between my eyebrows, a small invisible circle
spins. I put my hand to my forehead to check, its motion so
tangible, as strong as the hill's draw. Specks of quartz sparkle
in the moonlight.

Just shy of the summit, the Kanatawets set to work making
a fire in a hearth that, based on the pile of ashes surrounding
it, has been in use for a very long time. "Victoria? Please, come
closer." Malcolm's firm voice brings me back. He hands me
a metal cup full of tea. The fire crackles. We take a seat on
large flat rocks.

"How do you feel?" I feel well. I mention the sensation of a wheel spinning on my forehead. He asks his spouse to enlighten me. They both use the deep shaman tones that are so different from their usual voices.

"Beings chosen by the Bear Spirit are endowed with several gifts," the medicine woman tells me, "the gift of sight being one of them. What you feel on your forehead is what white people call the third eye, or what Buddhists call Brahma's cave or the Bear's Cave in our culture. Since your mother kept you from using your gift during daylight hours, you turned to it at night in your dreams. Nothing can stop you now from using your gift to help those who ask, either from the visible or invisible world."

I hear drumming. Yet Malcolm has only his cup in his hand. Gradually, the sound enters me and I become one with it. My vision blurs. Malcolm turns into a caribou with red antlers, then back into himself. As for Patricia, she transforms into a fat silky otter then, when I shake my head, back into a medicine woman. The shaman says, "Don't be afraid, you see our totems, just as we see yours. Let yourself go, trust in it, all will be well. The full moon will soon be out, we have to get ready."

Despite the gravity of the moment, my sense of humour kicks in. The image of a red-antlered caribou, a fat otter, and a blue bear sipping tea around a fire comes to mind! I try to stifle my laughter, but my shoulders begin to shake. Malcolm suggests I make sure to stretch my drumskin, giving me a friendly tap on the shoulder. His voice rumbles above the flames, "Hey now, this is serious stuff!"

"It's nerves," I say.

"No kidding!"

In the firelight, I watch his smile reveal the white of his teeth, which stand out clearly in the semi-darkness.

We resume our climb up the hill toward the cave's gaping entrance. In the moonlight, it looks like an eerie mouth open for a soundless howl. Using a flashlight, I inspect the cave that the Cree call the Hare's Cave. I see a recess in the back wall, probably bored by a hard rock during the last ice age. Its white surface, darkened by grey and black plaques of quartzite, reflects the light. The space could easily house a dozen people crouching. I raise my arms but still can't reach the vault. Here I stand in the heart of what was once, before it became a sacred site, a simple workshop for making arrowheads, scrapers, and other tools.

For now, all I can feel is the wheel spinning above my nose. The Kanatawets open up the inflatable mattresses and lay them down in a circle with the sleeping bags on top. The atmosphere cools and humidity penetrates my thick jacket. As a precaution, I pull on my wool tuque. Malcolm invites me to make myself comfortable. I roll up the unused part of my sleeping bag to make myself a cushion, my crossed legs hidden inside the rest of the bag. Malcolm lays out his sacred objects on a moose hide and invites me to do the same. The hide's smoky fragrance wafts through the air. My drum, tiny next to his, gives off deep vibrations despite the cold. We each have a Cree caribou-hide rattle, his handle is painted red, mine blue.

We've been playing our instruments for some ten minutes. Patricia turns on her flashlight, pulls out a notebook and pencil from her jacket pocket. This is the moment when, without moving a muscle, I feel myself projected outside my body. I stop drumming as does Malcolm, yet the cave still echoes like a huge heartbeat. It's lit by a turquoise-blue light. I'm back with the caribou and the otter, but now we've been joined by a crow. Noumoushoum Humbert! He appears inside my head, I don't utter a single word and yet we speak. Free of all emotion, I find myself at the heart of Life and my being dissolves into its surroundings. I feel as one with them. Our menagerie grows. Here's a red fox, a huge skunk, a moose, a golden eagle, and a grey wolf! I know none of them. Red Caribou tells me via telepathy that they have come to offer me their support and welcome me to the world of shamans. Gradually, glittering silhouettes appear around us. My conscious mind knows these are not human beings, that they are manifestations of the Great Mystery, unlike the animal shapes of Red Caribou and Silken Otter who are flesh and blood shamans.

Now I'm soaring like a bird above a wide river. I see the forest along its banks. Then a long banana-shaped island cleaving the water comes into view. Where it begins stands a monumental rock, split in two by frost damage. At the other end, three tiny islets face each other. Bulrushes grow in the water around the island as do sweet gale shrubs onshore. I hover a few metres above the ground across from the islets. I know Uncle George's skeleton lies here, in the earth under the sweet gale, covered every year a little more by the river's residue.

My mind grasps the Kanatawets' request. "Find a more specific detail, a landmark." Right away, I rise for a more elevated view. I calculate the islands' angle, then notice a lone birch tree on the big island, standing directly in line with the islet to the left. Between the two is the spot where I feel the bones' presence....

Sucked up by a violent draft, I find myself back in the cave across from Patricia and Malcolm. In the light thrown by the lamp, our breath's condensation hovers in front of us. The shaman lays his hand on my shoulder and, in his warm, deep voice that seems to come from a great distance, he says, "You've done a magnificent job! You're blessed, Victoria! Welcome to the fold."

Could it be that the handsome red-antlered Caribou has been moved by me? Reading my mind yet again, Patricia laughs with her husband. My conscious self seeks escape from the confines of my body. Malcolm says, "Hey! Stay with us. Victoria! We still need you!"

He helps me to my feet. My legs have stopped obeying me. What feels like thousands of ants nip at my feet and calves. I'm definitely back in my body now! I'll have to climb down the hill in this state since the Great Spirit's house is near the summit. Slowly, the Kanatawets fold the sleeping bags and roll up the mattresses. After the emotional cleansing ceremony, I felt totally drained. Here, now that the circulation has returned to my legs, I'm bursting with vitality as though fresh from a long night's sleep. Happiness glides inside me like an otter full to bursting with plump golden trout.

Having started the fire, Patricia serves us hot tea. We wolf down our sandwiches as though we are starving. The forest's silence encircles us and the radiant moon casts long shadows behind us. No one says a word, no sound makes it past my lips. Suddenly, I remember the red-antlered caribou in the dream during which I thought Humbert had appeared during our last night camping before we returned to Waskaganish. It had been Malcolm, Atik Nabeh, the Caribou Man, followed by his harem. A symbolic harem since most of his students are women. As though in answer to my thoughts, Kanatawet says, "We'll talk tomorrow. For now, we're going home to sleep."

Bathed in moonlight, diamond drops sparkle on the river's waves. We navigate in a motorized boat, light and easy to handle, that Malcolm transfers to the top of his 4-wheel drive jeep. Then we head toward the gravel road to Route 167 to Mistissini, leaving behind the Colline Blanche, the Témiscamie River, and huge Albanel Lake.

32

OFF TO NEMASKA
OCTOBER 2004

FOR TWO DAYS NOW, I've followed a crash course in wielding the Blue Bear's power. Patricia offered to guide me during my late-in-life shaman course. She advises me to practise my ceremonies every day and rehearse my power chant. I have to learn to master my power by grounding it in the body-nurturing energy of earth. Patricia claims I'm gifted. In a hurry to make up for lost time, I trust her completely.

By all accounts, I was a mystical child who prayed to the sun and moon whenever she felt the Great Spirit was no longer listening. In Catholic school, I grew attached to the Virgin Mary, finding her beautiful and kind. I wore blue to look like her. I often asked her for favours and never asked anything of her son, whose bleeding heart frightened me, and even less so of his father, represented either as a sinister-looking bearded old man or behind clouds surrounded by rays of light. Patricia says my totem has taken on the Virgin's colour. My mind created this entity, a symbol of my gifts: the Blue Bear Woman, an original way of uniting my two cultures.

The medicine woman insists on the detachment required when faced with the person asking for help. Referring to the way I lost control during the accident that led to Daniel's death, I ask her what attitude to adopt toward a loved one. "You'll learn," she says. "It comes with the grounding exercises and your ceremonies and meditation. One day, you'll encounter a situation that will call on your capacity for compassion. That day, if you manage to remain centred and effective, you will be a true medicine woman. But be compassionate with yourself first; don't ever exceed your limits. Ever. Always listen to the inner voice guiding you."

Knowing my brothers will arrive later that afternoon, I worry about everything I still have to learn. Patricia reassures me. "You're welcome to visit us whenever you want. We don't want you suffering from spiritual indigestion!"

The doorbell rings to our peals of laughter. Maikan's prying eyes peering through the windowpane in the front door make me smile. Behind him, Édouard's attitude is more reserved. "Welcome," Patricia says in English. Malcolm comes up behind his wife. Despite their own height and slender build, my brothers are visibly impressed by the shaman's imposing presence and beauty. After introductions all round, Édouard says to me, "We have a surprise for you. Go have a look in the truck."

As I step onto the verandah, I catch sight of Mouski's pointed ears in the passenger seat. With a cry of joy, I race down the few steps and to the jeep. Ours is a boisterous reunion. My dog squeals against my neck, nudging his muzzle into my loose hair. How I've missed this mutt! My brothers and the Kanatawets have a good chuckle seeing us so happy. Proud of his surprise, Maikan laughs till he cries watching Mouski do a few of his signature twirls in mid-air.

The next day after a hearty breakfast, we get ready to leave for Nemaska as Mouski turns on the charm for Clarisse, who adores him. We have to cover the four hundred kilometres of gravel road in five hours because of a scheduled appointment with Sydney Voyageur, the Nadostin project coordinator. Before contacting my second cousin Stanley, I want to keep the promise I made to David Fraser. Clarisse kisses us goodbye, "I'll see you in three or four days' time, right?"

Quite the optimist, that one! We stop in at the Kanatawets to take our leave. I thank them for healing me, for the ceremony in the White Cave, and for their teachings. Malcolm shakes his handsome head, signals for me to stop. Patricia hands me a ribbon-wrapped box that I hurry to open. My mouth gaping, I find inside a magnificent turquoise and lapis-lazuli stone necklace with a silver-encased stylized bear pendant. I'm flabbergasted. "I found it in a store in Sedona, Arizona. I think it was meant for you," Patricia says.

She then holds out the notebook she used in the cave. I read the description of the spot where my great-uncle George's skeleton is to be found. Without the two of us exchanging a word, she'd been able to transcribe all those details as they surfaced in my mind. "I thought this could help your second cousins locate the island on the maps they surely have. Unless they know the trapper whose territory it is."

To save time, I decide to phone Stanley right away and describe the spot on the Rupert River that I flew over during my vision quest.

We drive along the north road that connects Route 167 to James Bay. My brothers are used to taking it every winter during caribou hunting season. There are so many herds crossing at that time, they bring traffic to a halt. A windfall for hunters. The winding road is wide and well-maintained. In the front seat, Édouard and Albert keep silent. Mouski sleeps at my side curled into a ball. I left my car at Clarisse's so I'll have to come back the same way.

A CD plays Bach concertos in the background. The music takes me back to the mornings of our childhood and youth. When my father was away, we'd listen to Elvis Presley and country music with Maman, but on weekend mornings, Papa introduced us to classical music as he flipped buckwheat crêpes on the wood stove heated to a perfect temperature. We'd finish breakfast around ten, then, on sunny winter days, would put on warm clothes and follow my father on snowshoes along his trapline all the way to Christmas River. He carried little Makwa in his backpack. I brought up the rear behind Maikan whose short legs had trouble keeping up with his older siblings. Papa scheduled frequent stops to let him make his way to the front. Demsy and Philou would take advantage of the lull to pass their father, but were quickly put off by the arduous task of breaking trail through the thick snow.

One day, having left his rifle behind, Papa had to use a brass wire to string up a lynx, still alive, its paw broken by one of his traps, by the neck. My brothers were mesmerized by the lessons on trapping. I suffered with the magnificent creature and accompanied the thrashing of its death throes. Seated on a log with my back to the scene, I could hear my younger siblings' excited cries. I moved further away, claiming I had to build a fire for tea.

"We're here!" Maikan's cry pulls me from my thoughts. Ahead of us lies a long stretch of sand between two bodies of water. We can see a tipi-shaped structure. Nemaska's roads are made of fine sand. We head for the Band Council's buildings, easy to find thanks to signs pointing the way. The secretary leads us to Sydney Voyageur's office. He's a man in his twenties whose eyes sparkle with devilment.

"So you've come to dig with David? Before long, the banks of the Eastmain'll look like Swiss cheese and it'll be his fault!"

He suggests we go together to the restaurant to meet Noah Wapachee, the guide responsible for taking us to the archeological dig. We will be able to leave right away, everything is ready. That way we'll reach the research scientists by twilight. He checks that we each have a sleeping bag, the only thing lacking onsite for our comfort. My brothers nod their approval. Let the expedition begin!

After over an hour's drive, we reach the future power station worksite. Despite Sydney's warning, we're still shocked by the devastated forest and the huge piles of rock and sand next to craters dug by giants.

Noah, our silent guide, has a sullen expression that makes him look like a large, grumpy bear. His attitude conveys his view of the plan to flood his ancestors' trapping and hunting territory. Still not speaking, he heads toward a bay of the Eastmain River where the motorboat waits that will take us to camp.

Our great-aunt Carolynn, our biological grandfather's sister, married a man whose last name was Wapachee. I ask if she and the guide are related. "*Nokomis ouskwèm,*" he says. His uncle's wife!

So thanks to life and its coincidences, we learn more about our elderly aunt, the last keeper of Grandfather Johnny's memory.

33

THE DIG
OCTOBER 2004

W E'VE BEEN PART of the camp's activities for several days now. The research team is led by an American anthropologist, Nathan Anderson, and by David. They lead two young Québécois archeologists and two Cree students. We set out every morning by motorboat to a promising dig site. Beneath layers of golden sand, they discover artefacts dating back hundreds of years. A square hole excavated in the ground reveals multiple strata, traces of ash from forest fires and cooking hearths. The evidence points to the site having been occupied by the Cree and their ancestors at least as long ago as five thousand years. David reckons that they camped here for centuries and even millennia before then.

While my brothers split their time between the dig and fishing, I walk along the shore or down mossy paths in the spruce forest with Mouski at my heels. The thought of Daniel brushes past me like a precious, faint perfume. The pain is gone, replaced by muted sorrow. I know he will always be etched in my memory. I take notes and draw in my red notebook. My favourite person is still Noah. I thirst for his silence, his ancestral memory of the river. When the rain comes, we find shelter under canvas sheets slung above the worksite. On days that are too cold and damp, we stay behind at the main camp reading in our woodstove-heated tents, or talking and drinking coffee or tea in the communal tent. We listen to the scientists discuss their discoveries and hypotheses. Mouski helps to liven up too-long days. Behind my back, the young archeologists amuse themselves offering him biscuit after biscuit. In cahoots with them, my dog stops chewing whenever I join the group. But once their laughter gives them away, a slightly shamefaced Mouski starts chewing again.

By the second week of October, we can feel Indian summer on its way. The first part of my job will soon be over; the time to create and write will come later. With David's consent, we head back to Nemaska with Noah. I take in the Eastmain's banks crowned with forests soon to be flooded by millions of cubic metres of water. I'm overcome with sorrow. Upon our arrival, only my brothers and I will stay behind since Noah has to return to camp, but before he does Maikan takes a picture of us all with Mouski. A rare occasion, Noah smiles. He gives me the address for Carolynn, his aunt by marriage.

We arrive in Nemaska around four in the afternoon. I suggest we visit our great-aunt. The starkness of the landscape around the homes in the village is striking. Carolynn's condo seems to surge out of nowhere, set as it is in the middle of a huge circle of sand. We knock. An elderly woman's frail voice responds, *"Pitcheg', ap'ihiguinou!"* After a few steps up, we're in the kitchen. A slight woman with grey hair, her back turned to us, stands at the kitchen sink. Maikan greets her. She turns around, not the least bit disconcerted, and asks, *"Awan tchi ah?"* Who are you?

She's wearing a powder-blue track suit. The contrast between her wrinkled features and the girlish pastel colour makes us smile. I introduce us in Cree since it seems to me she probably doesn't speak another language. She exclaims, surprised, *"Johnny osisimch! Te boueh ha? Planchish outwashimch?"*

The closer I look, the more I see a resemblance to Jimmy. He wasn't tall, his body slender and his features snub and round, like this great-aunt.

She has just made a rabbit stew that she invites us to share. Édouard asks if he can pick up anything for her at the market.

"Hey, hey!" she says, "*N'tapimin poukechagan.*" She sends him off for bread. On his return, he brings in two walleye from the morning's catch and offers them to Carolynn. She thanks him effusively. It's obvious that he has just become her favourite nephew. We bid her good-bye early that evening to make our way to the inn where Sydney Voyageur has booked us two rooms.

Solitude will do me good after a week spent sharing a tent with my brothers. I phone William Domind, Stanley's brother. A man's husky voice answers in English, "I'm expecting him tonight. He should be here soon." I ask him to tell Stanley we'll be in the inn's restaurant the next morning.

After patting Mouski one last time, I leave him in the jeep parked outside my room.

34

THE BONES
OCTOBER 2004

STANLEY INTRODUCES HIMSELF as we're drinking our first coffee of the day. He is accompanied by a man in a red ballcap. The man is the Cree trapper who owns the land we're interested in. His name is Eddy Métamescum. He looks down his nose at me, skeptical and curious. My cousin must have told him about our plan.... Seeing my embarrassment, Stanley rummages through a big front pocket in his pants to pull out a map.

"I checked the whole section of the Rupert River that winds through my grandfather's territory, there's no banana-shaped island. But look what I found on this detailed map of the north-east section." He spreads the map out on the table in the middle of all the coffee cups. He points at a spot much farther east of Weetigo Lake, the Dominds' former territory. The river looks quite wide at this spot, but the island definitely has an elongated shape.

"I don't know why my grandfather went that far, it's a two-day walk from his territory, maybe more. But I asked Eddy to come tell us about the site and explain how to get there."

His eyes mocking beneath his cap, Eddy can't decide what tack to take. He seems more interested in the curve of my breasts than in any information we'd like to get from him. I pull my notebook from my backpack. On one page, I draw from memory the shape of the island, the shattered rock to the west and the three islets to the east, particulars that don't show on the map. I add the birch tree for effect. Eddy has stopped smirking, astonished. In English, he says, "Yes, like that! How do you know all those details?"

Vexed, I reply, "I just know, Red Cap!"

Amused by the exchange, my brothers smile at me with affectionate eyes. Stanley gives me a conspiratorial wink. I can't stomach machos and Eddy gives me the creeps. Something in his air reminds me of an ex-lover, a European, who couldn't stop trumpeting that he'd got himself "an Indian," as though I was one of the porcelain dogs people collected at the time.

In any case, Eddy told the men the island was easy to reach. We have to get back onto the northern road to Chibougamau. At about kilometre 246, we'll cross the Rupert River. From there, we'll switch to the boat and keep navigating to the right to reach the spot where the river widens. It should take about three hours to reach our destination in a boat with a medium horsepower engine.

Watching the man's cocky self-assurance reminds me of the night I ferried the whole family home safe and sound, weaving fifty kilometres through the perils of Shabogama Lake and the Nottaway River. My parents, drunk, snored on the bottom of the barge. I'd just turned fourteen and had operated in survival mode for years already.

Everything moves quickly from then on. Stanley borrows his brother's boat that Maikan tows on the trailer behind his jeep. I get into my second cousin's van to have a moment alone with him to talk. Mouski settles down on the back seat like a good dog. We've brought food for several days, gardening tools, shovels, and a tent. Shirley sewed a big bag out of white canvas that she embroidered to carry the bones. Her gesture touches me. For the first time, I realize how much Stanley and his wife believe in this project. An inner voice warns me, "You're only the instrument, don't forget it!"

The Indian summer is alive with vibrant colours, an ideal time for an expedition. Given the heat, we're bare-armed in our T-shirts. But inside I'm shaking. At one point, a golden eagle flies above our boat. Sitting up front with the bags and the dog, I call on the spirit of my shaman friends. Slowly, the deep breathing I use for meditation takes over. Soon we'll be approaching the island whose silhouette is visible in the distance. I feel a gentle presence surrounding us. Noumoushoum George?

Stanley is cautious as he nears the bank. He steers the boat to a narrow sandy beach. My brothers and I keep a lookout for rocks underwater and guide our cousin, then we jump into the grasses and bulrushes to pull the boat ashore. Mouski paddles around, happy to be in the water.

As the men set up camp, I walk to the eastern tip of the island, anxious to locate the place where my great-uncle's bones lie. Sweet gale shrubs slow my progress. We'll have to cut them back or rip them out based on how deep their roots run. The bushes scratch my hands. How is it that I always forget to bring my work gloves! Reaching my destination after some twenty minutes, I recognize the spot. What a bizarre experience! A quick glance shows me where we'll start digging once the sweet gale has been removed. The lone birch spreads its branches against the blue of the sky, surrounded by stunted spruce trees. Mouski sniffs the ground.

I remember an event buried deep inside, one that terrified my mother and pushed her to put a stop to my psychic abilites. One night in a dream, I took to the sky to visit the village's general store. We were poor and I always wore pants. In my dream, I was rummaging through the newly arrived clothing for girls when I caught sight of a pretty dress on the model in the window. The next morning, I told Maman I wanted that dress from the store, blue and white with flowers embroidered on the top. She brushed me off, saying the winter clothing hadn't been removed yet from the display window. A few days later when she went shopping with my father, she saw the dress I'd described in the general store and brought it home with her, staring at me, terrified. She gave me that present in exchange for my silence. I was six.

Back with the men, I note their efficiency. Not only have they cleared a space for the tent, all is ready for our mattresses and sleeping bags. Modern tents can be set up in no time at all. Stanley breaks a trail to the boat. Édouard builds a firepit, laying stones in a circle. I grab my gloves from my backpack, pick up an axe, and set off to find dry wood for the fire. Dusk will fall in about two hours. We'll have lots of time to make a hot meal and settle in.

The makeshift campsite reminds me of our youth. Our parents would drop us off alone on a beach when Maman wanted a break. Papa rightly thought that we'd end up learning to get by in nature. I don't think they ever considered the potential dangers of the practice. They had absolute faith in my teenaged judgment and my capacity to look after my brothers. Today I shudder at the thought that one of them could have drowned and at the horrible guilt I'd have been saddled with. But Papa would come back for us, safe and sound, a week later.

Sitting silently around the fire, we admire the sun's last play of light on the horizon. Crouched at my side, Mouski begs for a biscuit. Our simple metal teapot shines in the flames. Maikan breaks the silence. "I tell ya', our big sister sure gets us mixed up in some crazy stuff! But we keep followin' and are happy to!"

I smile, reading the message that lies beneath his teasing: he's glad to spend this time with us. Stanley tells them what led him to be part of the quest. He talks about how I'd dreamt of Humbert Mistenapeo before I'd even met the man. Afterward, seeing the importance the shaman attached to the dream convinced him of its truth.

We'll see tomorrow, I think to myself.

They talk late into the night.

Tired, I wrap myself in my sleeping bag with my dog at my feet. We'll be a bit cramped and maybe too hot. To be on the safe side, I open a flap above my head. Before falling asleep, I hope that my cousin doesn't snore as much as the other two.

I can still hear a voice murmuring, but I don't recognize its Cree intonations. I open my eyes, but am no longer lying in my sleeping bag. No. I'm in a dream. I concentrate on the voice. Come from nowhere, it seems to be situated in my ear canal.

"I've been stumbling, exhausted, since daybreak. Fresh snow scattered fine and powdery across the crust hardened by an early spring leaves no trace of my footsteps, and my fatigue keeps me from seeing clearly. Dusk is already stealing over this unknown island. A bright light explodes overhead. Suddenly, for the second time today, I feel a pain in my heart as though it's just been attacked by a ferocious wolverine. Inside me, the dark poison of fear. Behind me, the pack of wolves drawing ever closer. The keen impression that I won't pull through. I, George, your great-uncle, a hunter and trapper since the dawn of my days, I know my road ends here. I kneel. I may have cried out, may have wept, but faintly. The pain in my chest tells me the effort is too great, radiating now down my arm and back. A prayer to Miste Man'dou on my lips, a chant that I picture strong and loud, my eyes raised to the strange light, I fall face first into the snow.... With our land emptied of game, the territory abandoned by animal spirits, our beaver traps empty. I had ventured out, walked for three more days to track signs of a herd of caribou...."

In this space where the absence of time holds him forever in this moment, I say, "Noumoushoum George, I've come to you just as you asked. I'm not alone, the spirit of several shamans accompanies me, now you can leave."

The star-dotted sky is rent by a dazzling light in the shape of an eagle, its wings spread wide. Its rays envelop our surroundings up to the banks of the Rupert River. A black shape ascends from the ground, hesitates for an instant then, showered with light, vanishes.

"Victoria, wake up!" My brother Albert shakes me by the

arms. His voice triggers my anxiety. We're outside the tent, Stanley's and Édouard's flashlights shining on us. I must have been sleepwalking. A common occurrence when I was a teenager, this time I'm taken by surprise. I'd been walking with George's spirit, watched by Mouski, who yapped to sound the alarm.

"I'm fine. I was dreaming of George; actually, he spoke to me. Or his spirit did. He'd hoped to find a herd of caribou. His heart gave out. He died of a heart attack ... fatigue, fear, cold, and hunger. Wolves were tracking him, there was no game left anywhere. But now he's gone."

I spoke quickly, still reeling from the shock of my dream.

"That's right," Stanley says. "That winter, Cree families were found dying of cold and starvation in their winter camp. Most survived by ice-fishing."

I'm shivering in the tracksuit I use as pyjamas. Stars shine overhead. Still dazzled by my vision, I murmur, "Sorry I woke you all, why don't we go back to our sleeping bags?"

Already in the groove after our week on the archeological dig with David and his archeologist colleagues, by ten the next day we're hard at work. Édouard strikes an object inside the perimeter staked out by Albert. Stanley rushes over and helps him unearth what looks like a rusted rifle. The soil is a mixture of black earth, clay, and sand. Nervous, our cousin says, "Grandfather must be nearby. Careful not to break his bones!"

We promise to do our best. I catch myself wondering what condition the skeleton will be in after more than fifty years. Maybe we'll return with only bits and pieces so small, even his skull, that they'll fit in our hands.

My brothers and our cousin resume working with a gentle touch. The dog keeps sniffing. Tugging on sweet gale, Édouard and Stanley uncover a long, yellowed shape striped with green mold that breaks when freed from the roots imprisoning it. Suspending all movement, our hearts pounding, we acknowledge this sacred moment with our wonder-tinged silence. Stanley falls to his knees before the mildewed bone, laughing through his tears. He whispers, "Noumoushoum ... Noumoushoum."

Maikan and Édouard give each other a high five. A crow's harsh cry interrupts the moment of grace. Half-crying, half-laughing, I call out to the bird perched on the tall birch tree, "*Wachiya, Noumoushoum Mistenapeo, tchi mieutan'ha?*"

"*Caw ... caw ... cawww!*" the crow replies, indifferent to the barking of my shepherd mutt.

35

THE SECRET
NOVEMBER 2004

SCREWING UP MY COURAGE with the first snowfall, I start clearing out Daniel's office on this Saturday. Despite an urge to keep a few rare and precious books from his collection that I'd offered to give to Maryse—his friend who teaches literature—I file the volumes in cardboard boxes. I do keep any with a writer's dedication to me. Slowly I empty the bookcases, leafing through works by my favourite authors. I linger over the torrid, sensual pages of *La robe rouge* by our friend and neighbour Laure St-Laurent. A note falls out. I watch the yellowed piece of paper flutter to the floor before picking it up.

"To the flame of the love we make ... M."

Incredulous, I stare at the words like so many bullets piercing me. I look for something to protect myself from being torn apart like some fragile fabric. The novel was published four years ago. Maryse's handwriting! Stunned, I collapse onto the footstool I use to reach books on the top shelves. My heart is racing like a panic-stricken hare inside the prison of my breast. I deny the reality of the anguish hashing me fine with its sharp pitiless blades. My thoughts race wildly like a herd stalked by wolves.... Good God! This can't be true! Maryse ... Maryse and Daniel? My good friend who hugged me saying, "I love you! Daniel's so lucky!"

I'm consumed with rage. What had Daniel tried to tell me, lying in the ditch, when I couldn't hear a thing because of those damn sirens? "*...Didn't tell all ... that love....*" Had he wanted to confess before dying? Every time he went to her place, claiming they had work to do, literary discussions, were they actually sleeping together? What a windfall for them all my out-of-town invitations—poetry readings, conferences on First Nations authors! Gorgeous Maryse, single and, in her own words, "incapable of finding herself a man." She'd borrowed my man, why would she bother looking elsewhere? I'm choked with fury.

My first impulse is to destroy each and every book and file on regional literature so patiently collected by Daniel. A childish impulse that I'm quick to repress since, knowing me, I'd be the only one to suffer. Slowly, the tornado inside dies down and its violent gusts taper off to be replaced by the salty waves of my sorrow. Crouched with my back to the wall, I grieve for the pathetic love I'd felt, thinking it perfect and unique, whose loss dug such a deep chasm that it frightened me at times. Behind the door, Mouski keeps up his whining. The poor dog is beside himself, alarmed at my sobbing. I am a desert of bitterness.

"My dog, let's walk."

His ears at half-mast, Mouski doesn't quite know how to respond. My aura worries him; he can tell there's something different about me. I pull on my jacket and the tuque Sibi knitted during less tumultous times. November's cold sweeps into my lungs, its contact reinvigorating. With long strides, I head to the far end of the territory, to the forest whose wisdom and silence have always been my saving grace no matter the blows blind fate has rained down on me. I know that on my return, I'll have found the words I need to confront Maryse and the others, who must have known about her affair with Daniel.

Staring at the phone, I still harbour the hope I might be wrong, that the affair took place well before Daniel and I were together. But Daniel would have told me. It's better to know. Maryse answers on the third ring. She exclaims she'd just been thinking about seeing me about the books.... My icy tone stops her short. I invite her to meet me in a café on the main street. On neutral ground.

Mouski is still on guard. He watches from the corner of his eye as I get ready to go into town. He doesn't bother wagging his tail the way he usually does when he senses a car ride coming. He'd rather keep his distance, I must give off a smell of sulphur. He stations himself on the porch and watches me leave without budging.

Seated by a window, Maryse is wearing an ochre sweater that sets fire to her red hair. Her face reveals nothing. Yet I sense that she has an inkling why we're meeting in this out-of-the-ordinary place. Not at her house or mine. Her posture betrays her discomfort. I lay the yellow note down in front of her. "Since when?"

Unsurprised, she gives it a glance then looks deep into my eyes. I can read there affection, vanity, and shame. Tears glisten. I lock down my heart and wait, glued to the chair. The server brings us two cups of coffee and beats a quick retreat. Her survival instinct must be as well-developed as my dog's.

"Since a long time ago...." At last, she makes up her mind to speak. Tells all in a hushed voice. How the free love generation went in for couple-swapping despite the shattered hearts. Their group of friends threw themselves into the movement headlong. "You must have been part of it, too, weren't you?" she asks. I remain ice-cold.

When Carmelle was expecting her first child, Daniel gave up his extramarital activities. He took his role as a father seriously. Couple swapping soon lost its attraction for a generation exposed to family responsibilities like their parents before them. "When Carmelle left him ten years ago, Daniel's heart was broken, really broken. He'd thought he'd live out his days with her, you know? At a party at Laure's one night, he and I made love. I should point out that everyone was partying hard that night." Between Daniel's various lovers, they resumed their lovemaking, as necessary as their years-long friendship.

Isn't there some saying that you never really know another person fully? Daniel shared my life for five years and I either saw nothing or didn't want to see. I imagine what his friends must have thought of me. I'm overcome with an urge to scream and yell. I head for the washroom, lock myself in. The mirror reflects the image of a raving lunatic. I splash my face with cold water and take several deep breaths. There's no choice but to follow this bullshit through to the end. Making especially sure that I don't go under, that I keep my mind clear, breathe. Think of Humbert, Malcolm, Patricia, and my father—secret, loyal guardians, the healers who will help get me back on my feet—but let's hope this is the last trial before my path continues.

Our cups have been refilled. I find passing comfort in the bitter, scorching coffee. Marye cries unashamedly, tears she wipes away with the sleeve of her sweater. A wave of compassion leads me to hold out a package of tissues to her that I've pulled from my purse. No matter her age, a child is suffering before my eyes. I can imagine what she's been through all these years. In love with a womanizer who falls unexpectedly for others, but never for her. She who deluded herself about her freedom and told herself lies about her affairs that led nowhere and involved zero commitment.

"When Daniel met you five years ago, it was never the same for me. It looked like he'd fallen hard, even though he denied it, claiming he felt no need to be faithful to you. Yet it would seem that's the first thing you told him after your first night together. That you wouldn't share ... his dick! Otherwise, you'd just be friends, nothing more. Since you didn't live together for that first year, we did, if you will, hook up a few times, but only a few despite my insistence. The note you discovered was after one such time. Laure had just published her book and I gave it to Daniel. He loved you and didn't want to lose you for anything in the world. He hadn't touched me for over four years but was always afraid that one day you'd find out the truth.... You can take such a hard line sometimes!"

A fearful glimmer in her eye.

"That's right," I say softly, "I do tend to protect myself too much at times.... But how do you explain the fact he didn't break up with you when I came onto the scene?"

Her answer is immediate, unequivocal. "Like you, to protect himself! Love is unmistakeable when it hits you. But that too can be frightening when you've already loved and lost once...."

Her suffering merges with my own, I lay my hand on hers. Her humanity touches me beyond my own wounded love, and the truth she's just disclosed dilutes any resentment I'd felt. That dark energy that sent both Mouski and the server fleeing. She smiles, her face—the colour of her red hair from all the crying—grows calm, her expression one of gentle sorrow. At last she's able to give free expression to her grief. We speak of Daniel, his qualities, his flaws, and of our love for him. Of what tormented him and the heavy silence of his that weighed on his life.

When I take my leave of Maryse, I'm buoyed with new vigour. A few kilometres from home, I veer off to Laure's house. I want to ensure her loyalty. She's about to take Tobi, her Newfoundland, out for a walk. Her daily regenerator as she calls it. Laure is a dynamo, always inventing words that she sets to paper. I keep pace with her, the dog running up ahead.

"Laure, did you know Maryse was sleeping with Daniel?"

She stops, grabs me by my coat sleeve and exclaims, "Where did you hear that?"

"It doesn't matter, Laure. Did you or did you not know?"

She looks at me with motherly eyes, not knowing just how her answer will change things between us. Yes, she did know as did all Daniel's friends.

"I've loved you for a long time, Victoria, who knows why! I love your humanity, your writing, and the suffering you manage to transcend. When I heard you were dating Daniel, I spoke to Maryse and asked her to stop fooling around with him. At one point, I asked Daniel pointblank if he was doing right by you. I know he knew what I meant. Listen, my love, it was up to him to tell you, not me, not Maryse, or anyone else. Do you understand?"

I sense she's on the verge of tears. I know from experience there's nothing else she could have done since I've been in a similar situation myself. I hug her to me and reassure her, "I understand. Maryse told me everything, it'll be okay! My friend, my sister, my little mother...."

Back home, Mouski watches from the snow-covered porch. He doesn't race ahead of the car as usual. He waits patiently. When I call out, he runs and leaps into the air, signalling his delirious joy. I nuzzle my face into his thick fur, he yaps happily.

I turn on the living room lamp. Clarisse must be back from work by now. I dial her number. In response to her calm, gentle voice, I hear myself say, "I'll need a place to stay between my upcoming trips. Does your invitation to share your house still stand?"

Then I phone the Kanatawets, hoping they're in Mistissini. As I listen to the ringing of the phone, Patricia's words come back to me, "You'll be a true medicine woman the day you stay centred in compassion."

I can't wait to tell her she can be proud of me—I have passed the test.

ACKNOWLEDGEMENTS

The translators would like to thank both Virginia Pesemapeo Bordeleau for her insightful answers to our questions, and Luciana Ricciutelli of Inanna Publications for entrusting us with the responsibility of bringing Virginia's seminal work to English-speaking readers.

Virginia Pesemapeo Bordeleau is an internationally-recognized visual artist and author of Cree origin. She has published three novels and two poetry collections in French. Born in Rapides-des-Cèdres in 1951, of a Cree mother and a mixed-heritage Québécois father, she holds a Fine Arts Baccalaureate and has participated in numerous exhibitions in Quebec, United States, Mexico, Denmark, and received several awards for her art. In 2007, she published her first novel, *Ourse Blue*. Her collection of poetry, *De rouge et de blanc* (2012), was awarded the Abitibi-Témiscamingue literary prize. Her subsequent novels include *L'amant du lac* (2013) and *L'enfant hiver* (2014). She lives in Abitibi, in northwest Quebec.

Susan Ouriou is an award-winning literary translator, fiction writer and conference interpreter. Among her co-translations is Virginia Pesemapeo Bordeleau's first novel published in translation, *Winter Child*, and Emmanuelle Walter's non-fiction book *Stolen Sisters: The Story of Two Missing Girls, Their Families and How Canada Has Failed Indigenous Women*, which was shortlisted for the Governor General's award for translation. An earlier translation, *Pieces of Me*, won that same award. She lives in Calgary, Alberta.

Christelle Morelli is a literary translator and teacher in Calgary's Francophone school system. She has translated works of poetry and fiction, including Virginia Pesemapeo Bordeleau's *Winter Child*, and was short-listed for the Governor General's translation award for *Stolen Sisters*. Born in France, she has lived in Quebec and Western Canada.